The
Presidential
Adversary

Neil Freischmidt

Edited by Nancy Freischmidt

Order this book online at www.trafford.com
or email orders@trafford.com

Most Trafford titles are also available at major online book retailers.

Printed in the United States of America.

ISBN: 978-1-4907-1336-6 (sc)
ISBN: 978-1-4907-1337-3 (e)

Trafford rev. 08/27/2013

 www.trafford.com

North America & international
toll-free: 1 888 232 4444 (USA & Canada)
fax: 812 355 4082

This book is dedicated first, to my Lord and savior Jesus Christ for coming to my rescue, then to my darling wife, Nancy, for her unwavering support and help in the creation of this book. Nancy is a treasure in my life. She made my life worth living.

PROLOGUE

I t was a warm spring day in the city of Washington, D.C. People from all over the country came to show support for their candidates. It was election time! The city was in a buzz.

For the first time it seemed the people had two young, fresh candidates making their run for the offices of President and Vice President of the United States.

In congress many new faces began to surface with promises of better solutions and changes that would help put America back to work again. The country was experiencing employment loss; companies were moving to other countries to avoid tax increases; and health care costs were soaring. Too many Americans, it seemed, thought change was needed and spirits were high for these two young senators.

Along the city was the great Potomac River surrounded by small public parks, which provided many forms of recreation for the citizens of Washington. Rock Creek Park, one of the local favorites, was holding it's annual miniature boat races. Craftsmen from all over the world were there to compete and try to win the $100,000 grand prize.

A small group of young college students gathered to watch the miniature boat races. Among those students were Esther James and fiancée, Marcus Holland, Vice Presidential candidate. Feeling the need to be alone, the two decided to take a walk away from their friends and escape the limelight of the media cameras. Marcus was the candidate favored to win with new mastermind, Lester McChellan, the Presidential running mate.

As the two escaped to the woods' edge, neither could have imagined what laid ahead for them and the devastation that was to befall the country.

CHAPTER 1

"What a beautiful day!" Esther smiled at her fiancée, Marcus, as they picked their way through the crowd, seeking a little solitude. This was no easy task. The miniature boat races, the excitement of the upcoming election, and the fact that Marcus was the VP candidate made their search for space and privacy like looking for a needle in the haystack.

"When I'm with you everyday is beautiful," Marcus replied.

Marcus was a young man filled with dreams. He had dreams of making a difference. Dreams of conquering a corrupt world, of setting to right those things that were dangerously wrong, and dreams of marrying Esther.

Esther was beautiful. One could almost say she was more beautiful on the inside than on the outside. She was strongly independently dependent. She knew herself and others well. Yes, she could definitely take care of herself but she wanted someone to protect her also. Marcus was that man. With his quick smile, firm voice and mastery of his own mind, Marcus was her man. He knew right from wrong, good from evil, and had compassion on those that weren't always sure if they did. As long as those that weren't sure were trying to find their way, there was room for error. However, those that knew they were doing wrong and made no attempt at correcting their errors, were sure to earn Marcus' anger.

The sun was shining and a soft breeze played with the wisps of hair that had broken free from the capture of Esther's ponytail holder. Finally, as if by the wave of some magic scepter, Esther and Marcus found a small path to stroll away from the noise and smell of hotdogs, candy and sweat. The air smelled green and a little musky from the pond. It was quiet but for the whispers of nature about them. The beauty of the day was marred only by the crush of people, the flash of lights from cameras and the ever-present microphone being thrust beneath their noses.

"Are we ever going to have a chance to be alone, truly alone?" The question was an honest one, spoken with longing and sadness.

Taking her hand gently, as if it were going to shatter into a million pieces, Marcus smiled, saying softly and with a warm voice, "I love you and will always love you. I know times are tough and probably will get tougher but, I know, when this election is over, we can be together forever!" Softly, gently smiling back at Marcus she squeezed his hand and they begin to walk slowly through the woods.

The irritating sound of his cell phone broke the comfortable silence that had fallen between them. Marcus was met with a stony gaze from Esther as he retrieved the phone from his pocket.

"Yes?" the curtness of Marcus' response took Esther by surprise. This was supposed to be a day for them. Limited communication with the campaign was on the agenda. They had been assured of this. Now, here was someone, once again, stealing their time away. "What is so important that this couldn't wait?"

The voice on the phone sounded anxious. Feeling like an outsider, Esther moved away, not wanting to be part of what surely sounded like an angry confrontation. After many acridly spoken responses, Marcus closed his phone with perhaps a little more force than was needed.

"I need to leave. I'm needed back at campaign headquarters. I can't explain why. You'll just have to trust me." His voice was at once apologetic and angry. She could tell that he was visibly torn and this upset her. Why couldn't they handle something on their own? There was a presidential candidate to handle things also but, no, Marcus had to run and put out all the fires. Was this the way it was going to be for the next four years if he was successful? Sighing slightly, Esther looked at him with worry in her eyes. She knew he was capable of putting out a thousand fires at once but seeing him have to do so broke her heart. It seemed with each situation a little bit of him was used up. She worried that by the time the election was over, there wasn't going to be much of him left. She also knew this was her protective side talking. She dismissed her worry, opting for a more understanding spirit. Marcus and Esther walked to the end of the path holding hands. She snuggled her head into his shoulder and, quietly, without words, they reassured each other of their devotion and love.

A long, black limousine was moving slowly down the road in front of them. There seemed to be something ominous about the car but, then, sometimes Esther's imagination got the best of her. Still, she did have good intuition. Glancing toward Marcus all she could see was irritation and resolve on his face. Typical man. He was going to meet this challenge head-on and conquer it, sending it to the abyss, never to be heard from again. Her knight in shining armor!

Reaching the limo, neither she nor Marcus recognized the three gentlemen contained in the vehicle. The driver was seated, staring straight ahead, seemingly oblivious to his surroundings. Only one job was on his mind, driving the car. The other gentleman was rather large. Like a human block dressed in black. He moved rather fluidly for being so large. He seemed almost to glide from his seat to open the rear door for Marcus. The third man seemed strange. Though the windows were tinted, somehow he still should have had more of a shape. He seemed shapeless, almost as though he weren't solid. Esther once again just chalked all these thoughts up to her growing resentment toward the campaign people. Marcus also felt uneasy about this meeting. Who were these men and had he seen them before? Shaking so many hands and greeting vast crowds tends to cloud the memory.

"How are you going to get home? I don't want you to be jogging at this late hour. By the time you reach your house it will be pretty dark. Do you have someone to call?"

"Sure. A bunch of the gang will be waiting for the fireworks later. I can hitch a ride with them home. Now don't worry about me! Go and fight the good fight and call me when you get home."

"I love you for almost understanding!" The twinkle in his eye told her he understood and the warmth of his voice told her that he truly did love her. He gently put his arm around her and gave her a prolonged kiss on the cheek. Turning her around he gave her a gentle push to get her started down the path back to the crowds. Without that encouraging push, that gentle peck on the cheek threatened to become more than it should be at this point in time.

Reluctantly, Esther began back down the path. Turning to get one more glance at Marcus, Esther's eyes seemed to be deceiving her. As Marcus reached to shake the hand of the figure enveloped in the confines of the car, an ominous, inky darkness seemed to ooze over his hand and up his arm.

Although Esther was at least twenty feet from Marcus, there was no mistaking the look of confusion and pain rushing over his face. As if to confirm what her eyes were telling her, there came a shocked, horrific, growl emanating from deep within Marcus. In an instant he was pulled, almost sucked, into the car as if he were nothing more than a rag doll. The car started off down the road before the door could shut. The slamming sound of that door seemed to knock Esther out of a dream state. As the car raced off, Esther frantically started running after it. Only when her heart was pounding through her chest and there was no more air to breathe, did she stop running. Her fear and confusion were taking over where her brain should have been working. She was bent over clutching at her stomach when reasonable thought returned. Turning back down the road she once again began to run as if Marcus' life depended on it.

"Marcus, stop resisting. The pain will stop and all will be well." The voice sounded comforting and familiar. Something was very wrong. It seemed as though his body was being invaded, drowning in an oppressive blanket of hot, suffocating despondency.

"Marcus, please! Let yourself relax. The more you resist the longer and harder the process will be!"

Lester McChellan watched as his friend struggled against the invading evil spreading over his body. Soon the process would be complete.

CHAPTER 2

Ruth Foster was the first to see Esther bursting from the walking path. Disheveled and bleeding, Esther was gulping for air. Stumbling, her eyes burning with anger, she lurched toward Ruth.

"You've got to help!" Anguish, anger and the near loss of control were evident in Esther's voice.

"Good lord, what's wrong?" Ruth was near hysteria herself at the sight of her gentle friend in this condition.

"It's Marcus," came the gasping, desperate reply. "He needs our help. He's been abducted by something black. It ran up his arm and pulled him in the car. He's hurting. We've got to call the police. I ran but I couldn't catch the car so I ran back here. Don't just stand there, call the police, do something!"

"Fred! Fred Joiner!" Ruth screamed above the laughter and bleating of the crowd.

From several yards away Fred's head snapped toward the yelling of his name. Fred was a medium, non-descript man. He had brown hair, brown eyes, nothing to write home about except for his incredible capacity for loyalty. That is what drew people to Fred. He would defend his friends to a fault, trusting in what they said, assuming only the best of them.

He recognized Ruth's cry immediately. She had that take charge, commanding quality that would suit her well in her nursing career. She was a general, barking orders, demanding immediate action and trimming down anyone who did not jump to do her will. These were all qualities that would serve her well in her upcoming post at City Hospital.

"Fred, get over here quick!"

"I'm here, what's so . . ." Fred couldn't believe his eyes. "How, who, what's going on? Esther, what's happened? Your knees, your clothes, what have you done?"

"Stop yammering!" Ruth was gathering the heap that was Esther into her arms. "Get the car, we've got to get her home. None of these scrapes are bad enough for the hospital."

Esther was truly just crumpled into a heap. Ruth's arms felt safe and warm. Her commanding presence was reassuring after the awful sight she had just seen. What had just happened? Had Marcus truly been snatched before her eyes or was she just hallucinating?

Fred helped Ruth half carry Esther to the car. She was speaking so distraughtly that nothing seemed to make sense.

"I saw a black thing come out of the car. It just kind of floated out, over his hand and up his arm! It actually went over him, into him! Like it consumed him!" Esther began to cry uncontrollably. Ruth tenderly brought her into her arms and just held her. Esther began to repeat over and over, "Please tell me what's going on!"

Ruth looked at Fred and asked him to call the police. They had reached Esther's parents' home but her parents were out for the evening, probably enjoying the festivities of Election Day.

"Let her get some rest. If I call the police, who is going to believe all this babbling? Perhaps in the morning she may see things differently." Fred had never seen Esther like this before. She was so strong and levelheaded. Obviously, she had seen something but certainly nothing like she was describing.

This whole thing really troubled Ruth. Esther had the personality of a wild cat and was a natural leader. She knew Esther wasn't one to flip out, but her story was too weird. This was going to take more explanation.

CHAPTER 3

Clint and Mary James were just finishing up breakfast when their daughter, Esther, came gingerly down the stairs. She was still considerably sore from her injuries. Slowly, she made her way to the table and just as gingerly sat quietly next to her mother.

"What time is it?" her voice caught in her throat. It also was still sore from all the crying and shouting of the previous day.

Mary, a beautiful woman with a powerful but humble personality, slowly turned. Seeing her daughter, concern overshadowed her face. Not one for over reacting she said in her calmest voice, "Why not sit and have some breakfast? Anything you have to do can wait, nothing is all that important."

Clint put down his newspaper, and saw the rings around Esther's eyes from worry and lack of sleep.

"What's going on?"

Esther was filled with a great deal of worry and concern and it showed. Picking her words carefully, Esther began to explain what had happened the night before at the park with Marcus.

"They just took him, Dad. They grabbed him and just took him. I know he didn't want to go with them!"

"Now honey, Marcus is running for Vice President and is in great demand!" replied her father. The concern on his face was as evident as the concern on Mary's. "So, you really never know what is really going on. Things aren't always what they seem, and those secret service guys can be pretty scary."

Esther was beginning to think that perhaps she shouldn't be sharing this entire confusing tale with her parents. Perhaps her father was right. Things aren't always what they appear to be. After all, the black ooze simply could have been shadows. They were in the woods. There were a ton of trees; anything could have made those shadows.

If she went on like this, surely someone would start to think it would be better to put her away. Even though, she knew she had to investigate further. Deciding on this new course of action, Esther brightened her tone.

"Thanks for breakfast, Mom. Oh, come on! Get those long faces off. I'm sure Dad is right! If Marcus calls, please tell him I've gone over to Ruth's house. Bye Mom! Bye, Dad." Reaching for her coat she gave them both a hearty smile and a peck on the cheek.

Clint looked lovingly at his wife while calmly patting her hand. "She's got it bad!" Mary looked back into his eyes, concerned was evident on her face. Esther had never acted this way before and never would she make-up something like this unless something really strange did take place. Quietly and a little anxiously, Mary said a little prayer for her daughter.

CHAPTER 4

Clint and Mary owned and operated a small grocery store on East Main Street. Crime was high in this part of town. Most of the people living here were just getting by on what little money they made. Clint was now sixty years old and his health problems seemed to be increasing by the year.

"Hey, how are you doing these days?" The friendly greeting came from Barney, an elderly man who lived just down the block from the store. Barney Stein and Clint became friends over the years and enjoyed listening to Washington Senators baseball on the radio whenever possible.

"Clint I need a favor." Clint climbed down the small ladder he used for stocking shelves.

"Clint I need groceries and I just don't have the money To pay you." Barney was looking down, feeling more than a little embarrassed.

"Barney, you and I have been friends for years. We go to the same church and complain regularly to each other about the Senators. Groceries and money really don't matter between us!" With the wink of an eye, Clint helped him fill a bag of groceries. As they packed the bag full, Clint couldn't help but think that God has his hand on Barney; things are going to get better for him! If God can use me to accomplish His Will, then I'm privileged to do so.

"God bless you Clint and your whole family!" said Barney.

"Just go on home now before the butter melts!" The two men smiled and Barney went on his way.

Mary had been busy in the back room dusting shelves, organizing merchandise and eaves dropping. After hearing the front door close she moved to the doorway.

"Clint can you come here for a moment we need to have a talk." Clint recognized the tone in her voice immediately. This was a *talk* that they had discussed many times before. It wasn't a bad talk but sometimes you just didn't want to *talk* about it anymore. After all, it was his store too!

"Are you giving away the profits again?" Clint saw the smile and twinkle in her eyes. *Ah,* he thought, *it was going to be one of those kinds of talks. A little half-hearted scolding, a small lecture about being a wise businessman and then the good stuff, a little stockroom snuggling and kissing!* Clint looked lovingly at Mary.

"I just had to, it's what God would expect me to do. You wouldn't want me to ignore God!" Mary's smiles could be absolutely radiant. The love for her husband fairly bounced off her face. Sure, Clint had his faults but being miserly was not one of them. Still, she did have to monitor some of his kindness but where Barney was concerned even she would give him the shirt off her back, as long as he didn't mind pink Swiss dots!

Esther had just pulled up in front of Ruth's apartment house. It was 11:00 a.m. The morning had gone by swiftly. Mornings tend to do that if you don't get up until 9:00. Ringing the doorbell, Esther was trying to go back over the events of the previous day in her mind. Ruth answered the door with her usual "Good morning!"

Before she could continue, Esther started in.

"Thank you for helping me home last night, Ruth. I still don't know if any of it was real."

"Well before we get into all that, come in and sit down." Slowly Ruth turned toward the kitchen. Thank heaven she had made more than her usual eight cups of coffee. She had a feeling this was going to take more than one pot of coffee. Not wanting to talk about the events of yesterday quite yet, Ruth put down a plate of cookies and a hot cup of coffee before Esther.

"There are reports on TV that Mr. McChellan and Marcus are way in the lead and it looks like Marcus is going to be our next vice president! Wow, won't that be awesome?" From the stunned look on Esther's face, Ruth could tell that she was successful in taking her mind off of what Esther had really wanted to talk about.

For what seemed like the first time, Esther came to the realization that she could really become the wife of the Vice President of the United States. She and

Marcus had talked about this before but it had always been jokingly and in the terms of a dream somewhere far into the future. Quickly, her thoughts turned to her inadequacies. She began having doubts about what was coming. Would he still want me? Why would an important man like Marcus want to be seen with someone who's not so well refined!

From somewhere beyond the plate of cookies and cup of coffee, Esther heard Ruth. "Esther! Earth to Esther, come in Esther!"

Esther looked up at Ruth and smiled. It was a weak and uncertain smile. Ruth didn't miss much and she certainly saw that.

"It is all so wonderful but, Ruth, why hasn't he called me?"

"Why don't we call him?" Although Ruth's voice was light and upbeat, her thoughts were not. She was worried about Esther. Perhaps they should have addressed the subject of yesterday. Now it just seems as though she has piled more things to worry about on Esther's head.

Esther stood and started straightening out her dress almost compulsively. As if straightening her skirts would rub away some of the confusing and, quite frankly, frightening thoughts in her mind.

"I'm going to do something better than just call. I'm going down to campaign headquarters and see him to congratulate him in person, if you get my drift!" she said with a smile. Hopefully, she was sounding as bright as

Ruth was and she could erase some of the lines of worry on Ruth's face.

"Now that's my girl!" Ruth let out just the smallest breath of relief. Perhaps everything was going to be all right. Perhaps yesterday really was a dream. Perhaps all of this was just stress and tension. Perhaps, but could one really hope for that many perhaps'?

CHAPTER 5

Polls had closed across the country, but the final results were still being tabulated. Disputes seemed to have occurred in many of the states. It was being touted as the great "chad" debate.

At campaign headquarters all was a buzz. Campaign manager, Jill Rafferty, a middle-aged woman, who aligned herself with the extreme liberalists, paced back and forth, waiting for the call that would seal all their fates. Jill was a major force for the Democratic Party. She had helped defend the Roe vs. Wade project, as well as many other pro-choice issues throughout the country. Jill was a mover and shaker. If support was needed for a cause, she was the support you wanted. She had Washington around her finger. She was owed so much by so many, that those she came too almost immediately acquiesced to her *in case* they had forgotten something that she had once done for them.

This had been her toughest and most important project of all, making Lester McChellan the next President of the

United States! Jill was exhausted, yet she knew all the ballets hadn't been turned in yet.

"Make sure you keep an eye on those figures!" she called from her small desk on the balcony. The location of her desk seemed to suit her. She could hover over all the action. She was the puppet master, making the decisions and watching her will this, then making it become reality.

Lester McChellan strolled down the isle, as if he were without a care in the world. Jill watched him almost in awe. She had worked with many politicians during her career, making and breaking them but never had she worked with such a cool customer. It was as if he knew something she didn't. As if he had an ace in the hole no one but he knew about. At times it was unsettling. She normally was the cool customer but he was icy compared to her!

"Jill how are we holding up?" called Lester from the floor. He was walking around the room patting workers on the back, thanking those that had spent the night laboring over the press releases that would be needing to go out and those that arrived early with fresh coffee and breakfast for those that were there.

"We are holding our own and everything is looking great. I really believe that we're on our way to the Whitehouse. Hope you're packed up!" Jill knew they were going to win. All the propaganda that barraged the airwaves was worth it. Lester McChellan and Marcus Holland were the hope of the people. They would change everything. They were the future. Jill had done her job and, if she must say so herself, she had done it all by herself.

Excitement was growing at headquarters. Numbers were being reported from all the States. McChellan and Holland totals were rising. As the voting results were pouring in, so were the well wishers. The building was becoming hot and sweaty with the amount of people packing in through the doors. One of those people was Fred Joiner.

Fred had decided to stop and see if he could get a moment alone with Marcus. He knew that it would be difficult but he had to at least give it a try. Fred had telephoned Ruth before making his way down to campaign headquarters to get an update on Esther's condition. He knew that Ruth was the first person Esther would go to. Ruth had informed Fred that Marcus had not even attempted to call Esther the entire evening, nor did he try calling her that morning and, to Fred's way of thinking, that just wasn't right.

As Fred pushed his way through the throng of people, he noticed some rather large men standing on the perimeters of the crowd. They were intimidating to say the least. Fred was determined to see Marcus. It was that look of determination and intensity that caught Jill Rafferty's eye.

"Hello! I'm Jill Rafferty, campaign manager. I noticed you from high on my perch in the balcony. You seem to be on a mission!" she was wearing a cute likeable smile that somehow did not match her demeanor.

"My name is Fred Joiner. I'm here to see Marcus. I know he has to be busy with the campaign and all, but this is quite important."

Jill eyed Fred up. There actually did seem to be something on his mind. Security was tight here at headquarters. There were a lot of people who didn't want change. At least, not the way it was being served up. Fred seemed legitimate, not like some of the crazies that had come in demanding to speak to the candidates.

Fred, seeing that she was sizing him up, felt some further explanation was needed.

"I'm an old friend of Marcus'. I, uh, know his fiancé and, well, she was kind of worried about him so I thought I would come by and talk to him for a minute." Fred stuttered. He didn't mean to tell her all this but it kind of tumbled out of his mouth.

"Oh, I see." Jill didn't like getting into messy situations between candidates, wives and girlfriends. The less she knew about candidates' personal situations, the more effective she could be as a campaign manager. She reached for a phone that seemed to appear out of nowhere and began dialing.

"Hello, Marcus? There is a young man down here wishing to see you." There was a smile on Jill's lips but it didn't reach her eyes. Hanging up the phone, she turned back to Fred. "Marcus will be right down."

Marcus appeared shortly. His face was flushed. Whether it was from the excitement of the moment or from the oppressive heat of the room was difficult to tell.

"Good to see you friend. Kind of exciting around here don't you think? How are you? It's been such a long time!"

Fred was puzzled. '*A long time?*' It was just yesterday! He was acting like they hadn't seen each other for years! Fred looked at Marcus for a moment.

"Are you feeling well?" Fred tried to sound as if he was joking but concern was evident in his voice. "After all, it was only yesterday that we were all in the park together celebrating Election Day."

Marcus looked at Fred and, as if a switch had been thrown somewhere, his attitude had taken a totally different tone. "I'm fine Fred. How about some coffee?"

"Sure, Marcus. Look, I need to talk to you about something important." Fred's demeanor had changed now too. If Marcus wanted to be all business, then that was how it would be.

Noting the change in Fred, the tension between the two men seemed to explode. "How can I help you, Mr. Joiner?"

"Marcus, it's me, Fred. You know, your friend! Look, it's about Esther. She's extremely worried about you! She's made numerous attempts to call you on your cell phone! Marcus, why don't you get back to her?" Fred had abandoned his attempt at being all business. He was far too emotional for that.

"Mr. Joiner, let me make one thing clear. This is a very intense time for the country. We all have to put aside some of our personnel lives if we are going to make the changes needed. Families like the James, simply put, will have to recognize the fact that things are going to have to be necessarily different or they just won't fit in! Believing in childish illusions like praying to a God for financial help or to meet *real* needs, won't cut it anymore. I believe in reality! To align myself with someone that believes in anything but reality would be political suicide."

"But Marcus, Esther loves you! Please!' Fred's mind was reeling. This wasn't the Marcus of yesterday!

With sarcasm dripping from his voice, Marcus scoffed, "Love! What does a little girl know about love?" Wearily, he continued, "Please let her know it's over!"

This was too much for Fred to handle! With anger seething from every pour in his body Fred could barely contain himself. "No, I'm not your errand boy. You may become high and mighty but I think that is something you should do for yourself! Or, if you have really become that cowardly, perhaps you could send your campaign manager, Ms. Rafferty, with a note!"

Jill Rafferty had noticed the exchange between these two "old friends" and it did not seem as friendly as it should have been on this happy day.

"Mr. Joiner," Jill couldn't keep her nose out of this because Fred seemed like such a good fellow, "you know emotions are running extremely high today. I'm sure that's what has Marcus feeling out of sorts. Perhaps if you called on him after the final counts are in and he has a chance to collect himself, things will be better."

Fred looked at her almost sympathetically. She didn't seem to know the Marcus that he once knew. This fellow that he had just talked to definitely was not the same Marcus that was pre-election Marcus. What had happened to that one? It was all just a little too confusing.

As Fred pushed past the now frenzied crowd he finally reached the crowded sidewalk. There was a deafening cheer that went up from deep within the bellies of all those fanatic people. It was official. Lester McChellan won the election! He was now the new President of the United States and Marcus Holland the new Vice President! There was much celebration, people were hugging and dancing everywhere. Fred was trying to reach the street but people kept blocking the way. Suddenly, an elderly woman grabbed his arm and began to dance with him. Fred went along with her for a short time, turning around and around, until he thought he would upchuck. The conversation with Marcus had taken quite a lot out of him. Stopping so abruptly that the old lady nearly flew through the large glass window in front of them, Fred had nearly slammed into Lester McChellan, the new President! Fred could only mumble, "I, I'm, um, sir . . ."

McChellan looked at Fred with wary eyes. "Well, I'm so glad that you're in a partying mood. After seeing you and Marcus talking, I thought perhaps you wouldn't be." McChellan's words seemed warm on the outside but like a microwave hotdog, the inside of his words were cold and icy. There seemed to be something almost sinister about him. Lester McChellan held out his hand.

Fred's first response was to flee but McChellan's eyes seemed to bore into him anchoring him to the sidewalk. Automatically, Fred held out his hand to shake the President's. As their hands lock, a black shadow creature moved like smoke from McChellan's hand onto Fred's. In a matter of seconds, it completely entered into Fred's body, as it had with Marcus. Fred stopped laughing and just stood with his face looking stone cold. No emotion crossed the barrier that swept over Fred. Lester McChellan leaned forward slightly and, as if sharing a private joke with him, whispered, "Welcome aboard."

Anxiety was among the mix of emotions that Esther was feeling as she pulled into the parking structure for the campaign headquarters. Her mind was racing along with her heart. Marcus would surely be at the headquarters! She hadn't seen or talked to him since the strangeness of yesterday. She just needed to see him to assure herself that all was well.

Getting out of her car, Esther was accosted by a strange sensation. What was she seeing? It looked as if the building was moving! She must not have eaten enough breakfast or maybe she was dehydrated from the stress she had been under since yesterday. Slowly, Esther walked closer to the building. Looking up, what she saw amazed and scared her.

A mass of black shadow like creatures was swirling around the building. It was as if the building was engulfed in a whirlpool of black smoke. Surely, this wasn't real! Esther closed her eyes and opened them again with a pop! No, it was still there. 'It', seemed like the right adjective to describe this apparition. Somehow this black smoke gave the impression that it had a personality, an ominous, dark and evil personality.

Crossing the street to the front of the building, Esther felt as if she had to force her way through wisps of darkness. Finally, reaching inside the building, she was met by Jill.

"I'm here to see Marcus Holland." It sounded more like a demand rather than a request even to her ears.

"I'm sorry but, Mr. Holland and Mr. McChellan are gathered for a press conference and I really *cannot* disturb them." Jill's voice was kind but very firm. Nothing was going to move her.

"I need to see him *now*!" Her voice was rising at an alarming rate. So much so that the crowd around her had become silent.

"I know, however . . ."

"I said *NOW*!" This last statement was so loud that it almost echoed even among the noise of the still celebrating crowd.

Marcus recognized the high-pitched, stressed voice as that of Esther. Annoyance and disgust flared in his eyes. Heading rapidly for the staircase he bounded down the steps two-by-two. He made it to Esther with astounding speed and, just as quickly, he grabbed her by the upper arm.

"I'll take care of this!" he growled through clenched teeth.

Esther was astonished, frightened and horrified by Marcus' actions. He had never been rough or rude to her. His grip was hard and hurtful. His anger surrounded him like a coat.

"Marcus . . ." her voice was frightened and pleading.

Cutting her off before she could whimper out anymore foolishness, "I'm afraid that you are obviously too immature to understand the importance of this moment. As you seem so ill equipped to manage the post that you would have taken as my wife, I suggest that we should rethink our future together. At this point, frankly, I do not think we have one."

Esther found herself being pushed through the front doors and out onto the sidewalk. Tears began to burn in heavy rivulets down her face. What had happened? Where had all this hate come from? She stumbled and bounced off the crowds and fell to the ground. Esther sat hurt with a mind full of dreams that were shattered. She felt alone and frightened. Her mind just swirled around and around never stopping on just one thought. When they did, each reminded her of what could have been! So she sat and wept until she couldn't anymore. She tried to clear her vision. Wiping her eyes she glanced skyward. It seemed as though two of the shadows surrounding the building were swooping down around her. She looked confusedly at her feet. There, as if made of dry ice smoke, the darkness hovered around her legs, barely brushing her but not quite touching her. Kicking, though not really shackled by the smoke, she let out a small cry.

"Do you see this?" She grabbed at a woman waiting to catch a glimpse of the newly elected officials.

"See what?" the woman was irritated that her attention was being demanded by an obviously crazy woman. Hadn't she been the woman that Holland had just thrown out himself!

Just then a van pulled up. Four young people came tumbling out. Their laughter was that of those who must have had a little too much celebration. Bottles of champagne were being clutched and drunk from, not to mention, liberally spilled on the street.

Franticly Esther ran toward them. She must warn them about the creatures around the building!

"Run! Get back in your van! Don't go near the building! The creature may hurt you!" Esther was hysterical now. Marcus was transformed into someone she didn't recognize and although she had no proof, she knew that these black shadows had a hand in that. She didn't want anyone else to be infected. They were still clinging to her feet but did not seem to be able to attach themselves to her.

Startled, one of the young men dropped his bottle of champagne onto the cement. It broke into a hundred pieces, pouring the golden liquid down the gutter. Angrily he looked up at Esther, "What? Are you insane?"

he yelled in a drunken stupor. "Get out of here before I call security."

Pulling his arm, not wanting their jovial mood to suffer, a female companion whispered in his ear, "Forget it! She's probably a member of the losing party."

The young man looked at Esther through bloodshot, angry eyes and, with a cynical voice, hissed out "Better luck next time sweetie."

The four had a good laugh and entered the building. Esther just stood there confused. What was going on? Am I going insane? Why didn't the shadows go after them? Why didn't they see the shadows?

Esther finally reached her car. She nearly collapsed into the front seat. She sat back trying to make sense of it all, upset and totally mystified.

She was exhausted through and through. It even hurt to breath. Her heart was pumping as if it were trying to push out sludge through her veins instead of blood. She cried. She was hurting and scared. The only thought that rang insistently through her mind was, "What am I going to do?"

Champaign was flowing like water. Hugs and kisses were exchanged with delight because their candidates won! Jill Rafferty sat back satisfied but exhausted. Now, maybe it's time for a vacation! She smiled softly, contentedly.

"Ms. Rafferty, our new president wishes to see you!" Jill knew that Lester was not the type of man to keep waiting. Jill grabbed her laptop and hurried to the new President's office.

"How can I help you Mr. President?" That had a nice ring to it, especially since Jill knew she was one of the major players that made it all happen for Lester McChellan.

"Let's get this media show underway. After all, I have a great deal to say to my people."

For an instant that statement seemed to alarm Jill. There was just something creepy about the way that he referred to the public as "his people." Jill dismissed it as nerves on her part. She was exhausted and stretched way beyond even her limits. She was bound to be a little too critical and edgy.

"Oh, excuse me, I mean the people." McChellan corrected himself after glimpsing the startled look in Jill's eyes. He stopped and looked over at Marcus. Both men broke out into laughter. Marcus had adjusted well to the change. Better than Lester had ever dreamed. Jill looked at them. These men seemed different some how. Now that the frenzy of the campaign was over, she saw them in a different light. It was almost as though she *really* saw them for the first time. She could only hope they were joking, but what a bad joke if that's what it was!

"Looks like the media is ready to start, sir. I think they are waiting for you and the Vice President. Would you like a little touch up before you begin? I believe they have brought a make-up artist with them." Jill, as always, was thinking of the small details.

"No, I don't think so. Well, on with the show!" What an odd way to put that, Jill thought.

CHAPTER 6

The door slammed open at James' grocery store. Esther had long since stopped crying. She was left with extreme anger and frustration. How dare Marcus talk to her that way after all she had put up with? His words of undying devotion seemed to bounce around her brain, ridiculing her for being naïve. What an ignorant fool she had been. He had used her. She was a necessary evil for him. When he needed a date, she was there. When he needed an excuse, she was there. How many times had her name been used when he *wanted something!*

Esther yelled, "Dad! Mom! Where are you!

Startled, Mary dropped a large carton of pickles. *Oh, that girl! She will be the death of me yet*! Looking at the growing pool of pickle juice at her feet, Mary was now the one who was frustrated!

"Esther Marie! I'm in the storeroom. What is all the shouting for and I'm pretty sure the door to the store opens easily enough that you don't have to jerk it off its hinges!"

Clint climbed down from a stool he used for stocking. "Whoa! I think the both of you need to calm down a little before this, whatever it is, blows up into something big." Clint was always the mediator. He had no idea what was happening but it seemed rather urgent to Esther. His daughter wasn't one to over react so whatever it was must be important.

"Mom, dad I need to talk!" The tears that had dissipated when anger took-over, were coming back. Esther didn't like feeling like a child running back to her parents, but she knew that she could and they would be there for her. The floodgates opened and Esther cried. Clint looked into his daughter's watery eyes and gently wiped tears from her cheeks. Softly he asked Esther what happened.

"I don't know how to tell you without sounding crazy!"

Mary became alarmed. Natural instinct took over.

"Esther, has someone hurt you? Have they done something to you? Stop crying for pity sake and talk to us!"

Clint shot a soft glance at Mary. He knew his Mary. She was ready to storm the castle at the least sign of someone giving Esther trouble. She could be rather fierce if the occasion presented itself! Clint gently held his daughter's shaking frame to his chest. "Just take a deep breath and steady yourself. Tell me sweetheart. You know that you can always tell us anything."

At 24, it was still comforting to be "daddy's little girl". Esther looked warmly into her father's eyes. She turned to reach for her mother's hand. The demons in her mind melted a little. Enough at least that she could talk instead of sob out her fears.

"I think I'm going insane. I went to see if Marcus was all right. We didn't even really get to talk. He just yelled at me and said that I wasn't fit to be his wife. He broke everything off without any explanation and shoved me out the door!" Once again, the tears were gone. Her voice was rising in anger.

"He just left me on the sidewalk and went back in the building. As soon as he was in the doors, something detached itself from the building and started swirling around my feet and legs. No one but me seemed to notice it! It was like it wanted to grab me but couldn't. It just hovered around my legs. It was creepy. No one else noticed it even when I pointed it out." Esther was beginning to sound like she was rambling. Clint looked at Mary and then at Esther. He could see his thoughts on Mary's face.

They had been in study with their Pastor and had discussed such happenings from around the country, perhaps even the world. The dark shadows Esther had described to them were nothing new. There had been reports of similar shadows in different places. Pastor had explained that in the last days, the days before the reappearance of Christ, many things would happen and many darker things would appear. Things that the world would try to explain away with talk of aliens and other natural phenomenon. It was hard to believe that these dark shadows could be touching their lives.

"Look, I'm just going to say it! They were like shadow creatures!" Esther stopped abruptly. Not because she heard gasps of amazement from her parents but because she was shocked by the "knowing" look they were exchanging.

Mary looked almost fearful. "Did you say shadow creatures?"

"Yes and its not the first time I saw them." Esther looked at both, and began to tell them of the shadow creature she saw at the limousine when Marcus was taken.

Clint sternly looked at Esther. "Are you sure honey? Why didn't you tell us about Marcus before?"

With a voice very timid, Esther answered that she didn't want to sound insane. She wasn't even sure what she saw the first time or if it was real, however, after today, she was pretty sure it was.

Mary, visibly shaken, was lost for words but not for long. "Clint, we need to talk with Pastor Hayes. I'll call him immediately. Esther, you need to tell all this to Pastor. It's very important that you tell him everything!"

Pastor Nathaniel Hayes, an African-American man in his forties, was napping. It was a beautiful Thursday afternoon. A most unusual Thursday, he was napping! Ordinarily, Pastor Hayes would be making the finishing touches to his Thursday evening bible study with the church but the Lord had spoken so clearly to him about the subject that it had literally written itself. He was the pastor of a small congregation at Christ's Sword United Pentecostal Church on Fillmore Street.

Crime was a problem in this section of town but people here hung together to help neighbors in need. Pastor Hayes was well known not only on Fillmore Street but around the surrounding neighborhoods as well. He was known to be a very sensitive man. He knew the Word of God inside and out and he lived it. Pastor Hayes was also known for his no nonsense type of preaching. It was straight from the bible. Everything was bible based from the worship to the preaching to the counseling. If scripture couldn't support it, it wasn't done in his church. He never sugar coated his words. He had the respect of his congregation and his community.

He answered his phone with his usual, "God bless, this is Pastor Hayes."

"Pastor, this is Clint James. Mary and I were wondering if you could see us. We need to talk to you immediately. I know Thursdays are busy, but its urgent." Clint's voice reflected just how urgent he felt it was.

"I'll make time now." Pastor Hayes knew the James' and knew that they were not reactionaries. If Clint and Mary needed to see him now, then now it would be.

Clint, returning to Mary and Esther, smiled as calmly as he could manage. His stomach was turning, and he was feeling a little woozy. "We need to go now. Pastor has a little time. You know how busy Thursdays are!"

A half-hour later, Pastor Hayes greeted them at the church doors.

"Clint, Mary, and this must be Esther. You have grown. Haven't seen you for a while!" Pastor Hayes was never one to skirt issues. Esther hadn't been coming with her parents, or by herself, for quite some time. Esther looked down at the ground for a moment then slowly looked up.

A sheepish smile spread across her lips, "I missed you too, Pastor!" After a short hug they all moved into a conference room.

"Well, as you don't have a lot of time, we'll get right to it." Pastor always appreciated this about Clint. Not one to waste time, Clint continued, "Esther has something to share with you, and we believe you'll understand our concern when you hear it!"

After carefully listening to everything Esther had to say, Pastor Hayes looked at Mary and Clint with an expression that Esther was quite sure of. It seemed that he was concerned, excited and contemplative all at the same time.

"Are you sure of what you saw? I believe you are, but I just have to be sure you are sure." Pastor didn't sound accusatory. He just wanted her to confirm everything.

"Yes." The reply was simple and straight forward. "Pastor Hayes, other people arrived there shortly after I did. It seemed as though they never saw the creatures. I thought that I was losing my mind!"

Pastor Hayes stood to his feet, "Esther that's how the creatures stay hidden. In the book of Romans 1: 21-25, Paul spoke of people who became confused because they didn't want to listen to truth. God let them believe their own foolish imaginations and their hearts were hardened and they were blinded to the things of God! You have to remember that after the book of Acts, the church was defined as those that had received baptism in Jesus' name and had received the gift of the Holy Ghost with the evidence of speaking in tongues. They knew the truth. Those that were confused were the ones that, even after all God had shown them, rejected it. I believe the reason that you were able to see the creatures at campaign headquarters is because you have the Holy Ghost."

All this was nothing new to Esther. She had received the Holy Ghost at an early age and had been brought up in the church. She knew the power of the Holy Ghost, and she knew that she had been denying that power for the last few years. You see, her church attendance, or lack thereof, was directly related to her desire to be more like the rest of her college friends. She was torn because she knew God was still calling her. She couldn't bring herself to ignore him. Esther still prayed everyday, listened when he talked to her and read her bible. Without regular church attendance it just wasn't the same.

"You may not have been acknowledging God but, I think, this will prove to you that Jesus is acknowledging you!" Pastor Hayes hit it on the head. His gaze was steady as he looked at the young woman seated across from him.

Mary and Clint looked meaningfully at one another. Both were thinking the same thing. God is great. His mercy endureth forever! They had been praying for a long time that Esther would come to her senses and re-embrace the truth that she knew and, at one time, loved with all her heart. To think that God would use a situation like this to wake her up was a little unsettling but, they had prayed, whatever it takes Lord!

Esther remained silent. She knew that he spoke the truth. As though Pastor Hayes was able to read her mind, he mercifully broke the silence, "I think the four of us should pray. I would like to lead the prayer, but if any of you can think of anything I leave out be sure to chime in."

It had been a short discussion, however, a very meaningful one. The James' and Pastor Hayes agreed. The congregation must be informed. The problem was how. Pastor didn't want to alarm everyone even though there was plenty to be alarmed about. It was decided that Clint would activate the church prayer chain and inform all the members that tonight's bible study would be cancelled in lieu of a church meeting. If they moved quickly this could be accomplished before this evening's service.

CHAPTER 7

S itting silently in the oval office President Alexander Dupree, a strong visionary, hung his head. There wasn't a lot of time for remorse. His presidency was at an end despite all of their efforts. He was truly worried about the nation. Things had started to come to an even keel and now there would be no time to really see his efforts payoff. Sure, unemployment was high, but it was leveling off. The war was still going on, but peace was beginning to take shape. The Congress and Senate seemed to be working in harmony for the first time in what seemed like 100 years, but he was now the proverbial "lame duck". This riled him. Lame duck, my foot! He had little time left and if they thought he was going to go out as a lamb they were crazy. With new resolve and fire, he folded his hands and began praying.

The press conference had begun. The new President and Vice President were all smiles and congeniality. Everything that they had worked for was finally here. There was never any doubt in McChellan's mind that it would happen. After all, a deal is a deal, even if you make it with the devil.

Watching the two men field questions, the answers seemed to be coming just a little too quickly to Jill. They were polished and smooth, almost as if they had been scripted. That was, of course, impossible because the results had only come in this morning. Jill had an unexplainably uneasy feeling. It was creeping over her like ivy on a wall. She should have been all smiles, but something didn't feel right.

She suddenly felt as though she needed a bath. Yes, a bath and some good sleep. She knew that things would continue here for quite sometime. Silently, she slipped out of the crush of people.

Making her way to her car was harder than she thought it would be. There were, if it were possible, even more people gathered outside the building than before. Pushing past inebriated partiers and overly flushed celebrants, Jill still felt as though something was clinging to her. It was like smoke from a cigarette. It seemed to surround her. Had Jill been able to see as well as feel, she would have been frightened. The creatures, which had previously only clung to the building, were now clinging to the well wishers.

Tendrils of black smoke intertwined within the crowd. Hands and feet were being bound. Eyes were being clouded and ears were being closed. A black film was pouring across the crowd, the smoke filling their lungs and mouths. It had begun.

CHAPTER 8

Dorothy Lemay, a women of 70 years, was busy cleaning the church pews. She usually collected bits of paper, scattered pens and used tissues after the Thursday night bible study. Boy, that had been quite a Thursday night meeting. She wasn't quite sure what to make out of it, but she trusted God and Pastor to get things straightened out! She enjoyed singing the old church songs she learned as a young girl. She was doing just that when the door to the sanctuary swung open. Pastor Hayes came in quickly, on his way to his office.

"Dorothy, please get your pencil and notepad and come quickly!" The urgency in his voice stunned her! She was also the church secretary. Pastor Hayes was normally so easy going and mild tempered that the manner of his request startled her.

"Yes, sir!" She normally didn't call him sir but for some reason his demeanor seemed to demand it.

She didn't know what was going on but it had to be something important. He seemed more like a general preparing for battle than a preacher.

"I suppose you'll want coffee too!"

At first he looked at her puzzled, then got the joke. A slow smile of appreciation for her sense of humor appeared on his face. Thank heaven, Dorothy thought, a little sign of normalcy.

"I'm sorry Dorothy, but this can't wait! First, here is a list of names from our youth group. Please call them and let them know that I want them to meet at the James' home. If they ask why, just tell them its important. That way, only the young people who are serious will show up. Second, call headquarters. I need an appointment with Brother Kent ASAP! Third, I'll take that coffee!"

These two old friends had a giggle. Dorothy returned in a minute with the coffee, then retreated to her office and began making the calls Pastor had requested. Pastor Hayes looked out into the tabernacle, "This is going to be a hard four years. The people are going to need God. Thank you Lord that you always seem to become even greater and meet our needs when we need you the most!" *Yes*, he thought, *God is always ready for the challenge but are we? It was a difficult question. Hopefully, the answer was yes.*

The weeks since the election seemed to be speeding by. Changes within the social structures began taking place faster than anyone could have imagined. New bills were being passed concerning prayer in schools and public places. What the government felt was a better understanding of the term; separation of church and state seemed totally biased toward the church. The Salvation Army was forced to close doors because of their

Christian views. This began a landslide of problems for the surrounding churches.

Pastor Hayes had been busy taking meetings with the men at headquarters. The James' had been a huge help rallying the church's various groups to prayer and fasting. Esther had become involved in the church again. It gave her purpose and hope for the future since her engagement to Marcus had ended so abruptly. Now she only thought of Marcus 20-30 times a day rather than 100 times. She had volunteered to head up the youth group going to the Whitehouse that day to attend the great celebration. They were becoming stronger by the hour. Prayer and fasting had increased and with that, so had the spiritual insight that came with it and she wanted more.

Things didn't seem so scary when they began to understand God's word and trusted in Him. Yes, eventually the world, was coming to an end. Jesus was coming back soon but it didn't frighten you if you are prepared. Greater joy was ahead. The promise of eternity with Jesus, the Lord and King of all!

Outside the Whitehouse thousands of people gathered to celebrate with their new President, Lester McChellan. There were some protesters, but the people loyal to McChellan out numbered them 100 to 1.

There were ribbons hanging from every tree and post available. Fireworks were exploding, bathing the earth below in the colors of the rainbow. The noise from cheering crowds, honking horns and bands blaring out rock and roll tunes was deafening. Celebrities from all over were arriving giving autographs, in support of the new President. The media congested every available inch of ground. Microphones, cords, cameras, lights, and news anchors yelling for makeup people seemed, in an odd way, to complete the chaotic mess. Shelly Cleveland, a reporter from BBS news, was among this circus.

"Man, this crowd is unbelievable. You'd think he was the king of the world, not just the President of the United States. Tom, can you help me with this?" Her microphone cord had taken on a life of its own and was ensnaring her like a fish caught in a net.

Tom Jacobs, Shelly's very able-bodied cameraman and all around 'guy Friday', was already working on freeing her.

They had, much to their own amazement, seemed to have grabbed a prime piece of real estate. Since they weren't traveling with an entourage of fifty people, so much for a big budget, she and Tom had nestled neatly between two larger competing networks.

"There," Tom shouted from behind her, "that's him coming now!"

Shelly threw him an irritated look. He had announced this so loud that all the other crews turned around and swarmed around them like locust over a wheat field. It was going to be harder then they thought, given their prime position, to get in close enough for a couple of one-on-one questions. After some pushing and negotiating, they finally reached a spot near the edge of the driveway.

A large black limo rolled slowly toward the Whitehouse. Finally, it came to a lazy stop in front of the throng of media. Slowly, the back door of the car opened and out stepped the customary secret service men. *They look even more expressionless than normal* Shelly thought to herself. Then came the big moment. President Lester McChellan, in all his glory, stepped out of the back seat, waiving and smiling to the adoring cheers of 'his' people.

Shelly and Tom were thrust forward due to the press of the crowd behind them. Shelly stumbled a little, but Tom caught her arm before she could plummet down onto the ground. Once she had achieved a fully vertical position, Shelly got a head-on view of the back seat of the car. It seemed to have been filled with smoke; dark, thick smoke.

Shelly was brought back to the here and now by a sharp, slightly painful, jab in her back. Tom was holding the camera, getting some great footage of the President.

"Ask a question, for the love of Pete!" Tom nearly broke her eardrum he had yelled it so loud.

Shelly's microphone was shoved almost squarely in the President's face.

"Mr. President, how do you feel at this precise moment?" yelled Shelly. Her brain felt as if it exploded. Here was the President practically eating her microphone and she asks a lame question like that! Her career, and the ending of said career, flashed before her eyes. In a twinkling of an eye the moment ended and both she and Tom were brushed away like annoying little gnats.

"How do you feel at this precise moment?" Tom asked in obvious disgust and anger. "What were you thinking? That was a moron question! Who are you? Where is the Shelly Cleveland that I know? How many opportunities like this do you think you'll get in a lifetime?"

She looked lamely at Tom. "I know, I know," she started to offer up weakly, "but, Tom, did you see what was in the back of the car?"

Tom stared back at her numbly. "The back of the car?" His voice was rising to a screechy pitch. "Gosh, no!," The sarcasm was dripping off his tongue like honey. "I was filming the President. You might recall that's what we get paid for? Me film, you interview?"

"I'm sorry, really, really sorry. It was just that the car was filled with something nasty. It was like it had engulfed him, and then he stepped out of it." Shelly tried desperately to explain her confusion at what she saw.

"Well, maybe, being elected President and all, he shot the wad on a cigar and smoked it on his way here."

It was futile. She had blown a chance in a lifetime, not only for herself, but for Tom also. Her sound bite and his footage would have been sensational. It could have been sold to every market in the world that couldn't afford to send representatives of their own to cover the President. Now, all anybody will remember is that beauty pageant question she had asked.

"Tom, I really am sorry. When we get back to the station, I'll take full responsibility and all the blame. Maybe your footage can still be used? A good voice over and some editing should do the trick." Shelly really did feel awful.

"Oh, never mind. If I got famous overnight, I wouldn't know what to do anyway. Let's just chalk this one up to firework smoke. I'm sure that's all you saw, and that probably just threw you off your game." Part of Tom really wanted to strangle her, but they had been through some pretty big scrapes together and this one would be no different.

CHAPTER 9

"Well, these past months have been busy!" Pastor Hayes was talking with Clint and Mary James. They had gathered at his office that day to get an update on his various meetings with headquarters.

"How was your trip?" Mary liked to start meetings off with pleasantries. Clint just sat quietly waiting to hear the news.

"Pastor!" Esther was standing at the back of the sanctuary. "I'm sorry to bother you, but the youth group has arrived. Where do you want me to put them?"

Pastor Hayes motioned toward the pews. "Why don't you all just take a seat in the first two pews? Thank you Esther for getting everyone together."

Thirteen young people came. The normal youth group was a little larger, but true to form, those that wanted to be used of God didn't hesitate to come.

Mary James looked over to see all the young people giving high fives, excited to know what Pastor Hayes had in store for them. She beamed with pride when she saw her Esther! Esther had been working hard with the young people. It had suited her well. She made many new friends, and they all seemed to look up to her. Mary looked over at her Pastor, "Thank you for using her."

"It's not me." Pastor replied, seeing the gratitude in her eyes, "It's God!"

"Everyone settle down, we have some serious business to discuss. As you know we have a new President." A low murmur arose from the group. Most of their parents had been voicing their disappointment about just that fact since the election. "Okay, that's enough. This isn't a political rally. I would like to ask you for your faithfulness. We have a great responsibility here. You all know that I don't really approve of protesting in the conventional form. However, we all know the power of prayer and fasting." Ears seemed to perk up. Eyes were steady on him. If he didn't feel like a bug under the microscope before, he did now.

"We are going to use that power. Starting this weekend, I would like you to split up into four groups. I am going to ask you for a commitment of at least four hours a day. I haven't worked out all the details yet, but my plan is to have a small group meet on the east side of the park across from the Whitehouse and pray. While that group is praying I would like the next group to be ready, perhaps gathering early and begin by singing some praise songs loud and joyful, you know, to warm up!' He was smiling. When the shifts are up, the next two groups will rotate in. We want to surround the Whitehouse with prayer. Before we can start this, we will need your parents' permission. I have a form they can sign. Now, this is serious business. I want it understood that we are not going to just be spending time in the park on a lovely day!"

Pastor's admonishment hadn't fallen on deaf ears. From his demeanor, the young people recognized that he truly was counting on them.

Saturday came quickly. Permission slips were handed in and the groups had been chosen. Clint and Mary had volunteered to be the official shuttle service to the park. They had packed up a small care package for each prayer warrior. Water bottles, fruit, crackers with peanut butter; not a lavish feast just something to sustain teenagers through four hours of prayer.

The small group was faithful in their prayer as was the group that relieved them. They prayed for the President; that God would use him to lead the country according to God's will. They prayed for his family; that God would protect them from evil and the influence of evil in their lives. They prayed similarly for the Vice President. Finally, they prayed for their country, which, seemingly was turning from God toward the sin of Solomon. The country was putting too many gods before the Lord God. Money, lust, humanism, and blind tolerance of varying beliefs and obvious sin was rampart in the name of accepting each other.

Their Pastor had carefully instructed them in the type of prayer but left it up to them to find their own words. "You pray for your enemy or those that you think would like to do you harm." Pastor had left his warning at that.

CHAPTER 10

Sitting in the Oval office, President McChellan summoned his Vice President Marcus Holland and invited him to join him at the large window behind his chair. Whenever he needed to take a time out he preferred to do so in front of the window. It had been a few months now since he took office. He had the landscape of the park across the street pretty well memorized.

"Marcus," there was an uneasy tone about his voice. Marcus had noticed this tone seeping into his voice whenever he was looking out the window. "Have you noticed that since I took office, there always seems to be a small group of young people under the tree across the way? It seems strange to me that they are there every morning, all day and into the evening. I know that at that age, I wouldn't have been spending all my day in the park. I get a strange feeling every time I see them." His voice trailed off.

Marcus was at his side now. Yes, he had noticed them and, yes, he also seemed to feel something strange when they were there.

They were not the only ones who had noticed this group of young people. People passing by were aware of them. As they sat praying, sharing scriptures and singing songs of praise, strangers would comment. Some strangers joined in for a bit. Some strangers merely jeered, shouted obscenities and moved away. Any way you looked at it, they were being noticed.

For Shelly Cleveland and Tom Jacobs, this was their next big news assignment. Since the inauguration incident, they had been picking up these human-interest assignments. At least this assignment had humans! Shelly and Tom were getting tired of cute kitties, drooling dogs and the zoo.

They arrived, camera in hand, just in time for the changing of the guard. Esther and her group were relieving the previous group. As the groups exchanged greetings and information about the progress of the day, Shelly and Tom introduced themselves.

"Excuse me," Shelly's tone was light and friendly, "do you mind if we talk to you?" Tom had already turned on the light for the camera and had it hoisted on his shoulder.

"Who's the leader of this little band?" Shelly had directed her question at no one in particular. It became clear to her that the young lady in the brown shirt and blue jean skirt was the leader. This description seemed odd only because, outside of the color of the different blouses and varying materials, all the girls in this group had skirts on. Come to think of it, they all had a similar look. Their faces were clear of make-up, they all had varying lengths of long hair and there was an obvious absence of jewelry. Similar looks but somehow totally different. The young men were dressed in long pants and shirts. One would have thought on such a warm day as this, at least one of them would have had shorts on or even a tank top. Shelly's interest was beginning to peak. There was something oddly familiar about this group.

"Can I help you?" Esther was more than a little weary of Shelly and her cameraman. This looked like trouble to her. Suddenly the thought of screaming 'stranger' and yelling for her mom and dad didn't seem so bad.

"Why sure!" again the light, friendly voice came. "Are you the leader?" Seeing Esther's discomfort, Shelly decided on another tact. "We have been hearing about your group from our viewers. People are interested in what you're doing here. Apparently, you have been standing vigil here everyday for about two weeks."

"Hey stranger!" Esther had never heard a voice sound so sweet! Ruth came strutting across the park, all smiles and sunshine. She arrived as if on cue! "What's all this about?" She waved her arm toward Shelly and Tom. "I don't see you for weeks and here I find you in the park stirring things up! I knew it had to be you! I heard there was a group of kids sitting in the park morning to night everyday and somehow I just knew you were at the center of it! I should be furious with you! You missed my graduation and haven't even talked to Fred and me since the Marcus thing!"

Shelly's ears perked up, 'the Marcus thing'? Now there seemed to be something more to this small group of pigeons.

"Hi! Let me introduce myself. I'm Shelly Cleveland and this is my cameraman, Tom Jacobs. Obviously, you know each other. I was just trying to get a handle on what's going on here."

Esther threw Ruth a warning look. Ruth, never one to back down to easily, faced Shelly full on, "And, just what do you think is going on here? As far as I know it isn't illegal to meet a group of friends at the park!"

Esther interrupted, hoping to avoid an escalating confrontation between her well-meaning friend and these news people.

"Look, I don't mean any harm. It's just a human-interest thing! Why are you getting so excited? Or, is there something more to this little group meeting?"

Esther decided to jump into the gap between these two, "I really don't mind talking about what's going on, it's just that with the camera and all, it's a little intimidating. Perhaps, if we could talk first, then you can get some footage or whatever you want."

Shelly finally took her eyes off Ruth and seemed to calm down a little. "Sure, I suppose we did come at you at little suddenly. I'm sorry, I missed your name, actually, both your names."

With the tension seeming to subside, Esther introduced herself and Ruth, explaining that Ruth and she were long time friends.

"Maybe we could all sit down at a table and talk."

After leading Shelly, Tom and Ruth to a nearby picnic table, Esther started very tentatively, to tell the tale of what events led up to the prayer meetings in the park.

Ruth's reaction was of anger. How could Marcus turn into such an ill-mannered boob! It was no wonder that Esther ran back to that church of hers. Although, when she thought of it, it did seem to have been the right thing for her.

Shelly's reaction was much different. Tom looked over at Shelly and for the first time since the Whitehouse incident, thought perhaps there was something to what Shelly had seen. He remained silent but very attentive.

"You say you saw something black around Holland, kind of engulfing him?"

"Well, yes."

"I don't want you to think that I'm patronizing you, but I think I saw the same thing you did. It was the night of the fireworks and jazz on the Whitehouse lawn. When the President got out of his limo. I told Tom about it but he didn't see anything and thought maybe it was just smoke from all the fireworks."

"Shelly, I don't mean to interrupt, but we are kind of on a deadline." Tom could see that this was something that Shelly wanted to discuss further, but they did have a story to do. "Why don't I shoot a clip of the kids praying or whatever, and you do a sound bite to go along with it. Then I'll wrap things up and take the truck back to the studio. That way, you can stay and talk with Esther and Ruth."

Shelly was thankful for a friend that could read her mind. She did the sound bite and helped Tom to pack up the truck. Waving to him, she returned to her new friends at the picnic table.

The afternoon seemed to have flown by. Shelly had asked a myriad of questions. She told more about herself to these strangers/friends than she had ever told anyone before. She explained that long ago her grandmother had taken her to church every Sunday. It sounded a lot like the church that Esther had described. Shelly had remembered things that she had forgotten about for ages. She remembered crying at the altar. She had spoken with "other tongues" as her grandmother had called it. She remembered the feeling of all consuming love as her grandmother cried and praised the Lord for the gift He had given her granddaughter. Grandma had taught her a great deal about those experiences, but as Shelly grew up and visited her grandmother less and less, the lessons had been lost.

It had been some time since Shelly had talked with anyone about those things. *I was so young she thought.* "*I would have believed anything.*" Shelly left the park thinking about the discussions she had with the little prayer vigil group in the park. Shelly really didn't understand all the supernatural stuff the women were talking about. She saw for herself the dark smoke they spoke of. If this was real it had a hold on the President. Shelly dealt only in facts not superstition. The women couldn't prove that the supernatural existed or, for that matter had control of the President, but Shelly knew, supernatural or not, something was wrong within the government. It was ugly and corrupt and it had a tight grip on every branch and at every level. Maybe by investigating the tips she has been receiving from her sources within the Whitehouse, she could inform the public and put an end to it. She knew that to many questions had been asked and blocked. Information had filtered out of offices that normally were watertight. Leads had suddenly dead-ended while some had mysteriously opened up all the more, stirring the drive within her to investigate deeper until the whole truth came out.

Driving down Washington Avenue, her cell phone began ringing.

"Hello, this is Shelly. Hi, Tom, What do you have?" Tom told her that an anonymous woman called with information about a secret meeting between Laurence Tillman and Jack Mason. Tillman was the President of Fedway, the nation's largest mortgage company. Mason was the President of Aztec Motors. What the two of them had to talk about was the big mystery.

"I can't explain over the phone just get to 2100 Maplewood Drive fast!"

"Wait a minute, Tom. What's going on? Are you in trouble?" The phone got very quiet, "Tom, are you still there?" she asked softly.

"Yeah, I'm all right, just trying to get my thoughts together. Shelly just get here!"

The urgency in his voice concerned her. Tom was pretty cool and collected. He had to be. Tom had covered wars, union strikes, and the major metro beat for over 20 years. If he thought it was urgent, it must be!

Shelly spotted the news van in the parking lot. She parked and made her way quickly to it. There seemed to be an awful lot of black suits wandering around. Earphone jacks and dark glasses were apparently the fashion statement for the day.

"That was fast!" he said, helping her into the van.

"O.K., Tom, what's up!" she was starting to get annoyed with all the secrecy.

Sensing her mood, Tom changed his tactics. Acting almost bored, he casually flipped on the video cam. "Not only did Tillman and Mason arrive, but Yuhma as well! You know the king of the Asian auto industry! If that's not interesting enough, Ashford showed up too!"

Shelly was truly awed at this news. In fact, she was speechless, not a virtue ever displayed by her.

"Ready for the biggest news? Vice President Holland is in there too!"

"What? This is too good! How many other stations know about this? I didn't see anyone's vans. How did you find out? Can we get in there? That's what all the secret service is about!" Words were spilling out of her mouth like water over a damn.

Placing his hand over her mouth "Slow down! I'm not sure if I even know all the answers! So far it looks like just you and me. I'd like to keep it that way. I told the suits we were doing a story about elm bugs eating trees. They seemed to buy it, so if we unpack some of our stuff they won't be suspicious."

"Tom, we need to find out what's going on! This is big! Why are all these heads of companies together, and what does our beloved VP have to say to them that's so secret it can't be said in the Whitehouse?"

"Their security is intense! If we take only the portable, smaller equipment and fake some footage by that clump of trees, we could duck into those bushes. From there, there's a chance at the kitchen door." Tom was getting that old tingling feeling of terror and intrigue that he had back in the war zones.

"Come on Tom let's go!"

The excitement was flushing Shelly's face. She was nearly breathless. Tom had seen this on other young reporters. It was dangerous but, then, sometimes ignorance made out where bravery stopped. "Let's see how far we can get before we get caught!" Her smile was infectious.

Tom, looking straight ahead, not wanting her to see his own eagerness, reluctantly agrees. "O.K., but if we get killed, it will be your fault!"

"This is our Pulitzer!"

"This could be our execution!"

Shelly planted a huge kiss on his cheek. "Come on, brave boy!" she laughs.

"It's been nice working with ya!"

Taking a deep, steadying breath, Shelly grabbed her microphone and in her best imitation of a bored reporter, she made for the clump of elms. Tom followed carrying only a small video camera. Shoved deep into his pockets were an extra battery pack and film cartridge. Those cheap idiots at the station still hadn't flipped for digital equipment.

Standing under the elms, Shelly eyed two secret service guys taking a little too much interest in them. "So far, so good!" she whispered in Tom's ear. "Unfortunately, it looks like we're getting company."

"Move under the tree and start talking!" Tom didn't like the look of these two. They weren't the two he had talked to earlier about the bugs. Getting an uneasy feeling, he turned his back on them deliberately. Maybe if he ignored them, they'd ignore him.

"What did you get me into!" he whispered back at Shelly with a touch of sarcasm.

"Excuse me," the voice sounded more like a command to attention, than a request, "what business do you have here?"

Shelly took the lead, "Why hello! We're from BBS. We're covering the bug infestation of the capital's elm trees. I know it's an important story, but I never suspected they'd send out the secret service!" Shelly had put just enough sass and sarcasm in her voice to be charming but not enough to be insulting. The effect was not lost on the agent.

Smiling a very small agreeable smile, he reacted to her charm. "Well, you know, the service is here to protect the United States from all types of terrorism, even to our trees!"

Knowing that she had chinked his cold armor, she dangerously pressed forward, "I know why I'm here, punishment, but, why is the secret service here? Perhaps there's a bigger story then the bugs?"

Tom nearly lost control of his bowels! Was she crazy? Hoping the trickling sweat from his back wasn't soaking through his shirt, he chimed in "You know these cocky young reporters! Always looking for the Pulitzer Prize winning story. Look, sweetie, it's awfully hot out and I'm starting to melt. Do you think we could get on with the bug thing so I can go grab a brew in a nice cool bar?"

"Sure," she turned and winked at the agent, "you know these crotchety old cameramen. Worn out and saggy. No time for anything but brew and broads!"

The exchange between them seemed to amuse the agent, however, he still had his job to do. "I appreciate both your points of view, but I'm going to have to do a quick pat down, if you don't mind." It wasn't really a request as much as a requirement, and they weren't going to dissuade him.

He started with Shelly. It was just a quick sweep, nothing much. She didn't have any pockets. After unscrewing the head of the microphone to make sure that it was a microphone, he gave her a real smile and turned his attention toward Tom. Tom's deep pockets were of great interest to him. Reaching into his right front pocket he pulled the battery pack and extra film cartridge out.

"I thought you two were here to do a quick story on bugs?" The smile was completely gone from his face. Suspicion clouded his eyes as his lids lowered to half-mast.

"As you can tell by the equipment, those penny pinching morons from the station aren't really concerned that this junk doesn't work half the time. I get to the middle of a story, even a lousy 5-minute bite, and this thing craps out on me. So, to avoid running back to the truck, I just keep an extra battery and film pack on me. It kinda goes back to the 'worn out and saggy old cameraman' image." Tom hoped that his voice didn't sound as shaky as his knees were feeling. Leavenworth had never seemed like a good vacation spot. Death by firing squad for treason didn't sound any better.

This guy really did seem a little unsteady. Maybe it was the heat. The girl was cute and not without her charms. Not wanting to appear too congenial the agent replied gruffly, "Just don't take too long."

Tom nearly let out a sigh of relief at the sound of the agent's earpiece. It made just the slightest of noise, turning the agent's attention to his sleeve. Speaking softly into his cuff, he glanced at Shelly and then at

Tom. Press people were a nuisance. Walking back to his partner, he just wanted to get this assignment over with. It was hot and babysitting a bunch of rich, over indulged businessmen wasn't what he signed on for. He was supposed to be protecting the Commander in Chief!

Shelly shot a glance at Tom as they both swiftly made for the bushes. The agent's back was still turned toward them as they ducked into the brush. The kitchen door was a mere sixty feet from them. The traffic coming in and out of the kitchen had been fairly steady. Groceries, drinks and ice were being delivered as if there were 500 men in there instead of five.

Providence was on their side. Having to open and shut the door was becoming bothersome. One of the deliverymen stooped to block it open. Not believing their luck, Shelly and Tom didn't hesitate to slip inside the door. Tom knew they were taking too many chances. They didn't know the layout of the house, the number of agent's inside the house or the whereabouts of the meeting room. They found themselves surrounded by boxes of supplies. It appeared as if this mudroom had been used for storage of some kind before today's meeting. Peering into the kitchen, there appeared to be only one cook. He was busy shouting at the deliverymen and pushing things around. That was good. The more frazzled he was the better. Shelly pulled on Tom's shirt nearly tumbling him to the floor. Another deliveryman was coming through the door. Trying to crouch into the cracks of the floor, the thud of a box being stacked onto the top the one they were hiding behind, nearly gave them both a heart attack.

After an eternity, the final delivery was made and the door was slammed firm and resolutely behind him. Shelly was busting to talk, she had to say something, but the look of warning in Tom's eyes told her if she made a peep, he would kill her. Motioning for her to stay close on his tail, Tom specked out the kitchen layout. There was a prep island in the center of the kitchen. Directly along the wall Tom was peering around was the stove. Simmering on the stove was a large stockpot along with various other pots. On the other side of the island, directly across from the stove, was the refrigerator. The only other door to the kitchen was at the end of the island. It appeared to lead into a hallway.

Turning once again to Shelly, the hand signals began. Shelly felt as if she were in a flag corps, only she didn't know the flags. Giving up, Tom got as close to her ear as possible, "I'm going to flip up the burners, when the pots boil over, duck for the island. No noise!"

Waiting until the cook had his head in the refrigerator, Tom stretched his arm for the stove knobs. Giving them all a firm flick, he ducked back into his hiding place. It was only a matter of seconds before confusion reigned. Pots lids went crashing to the floor, hissing and boiling sounds erupted, and the cook went into full-fledged panic.

Reaching behind him, grabbing any part of Shelly he could get a hold of, Tom literally dived for cover behind the island, dragging Shelly behind him. Before she could fully regain her balance in their new perch, he again pulled her abruptly into the hallway. Looking as if his head was on a swivel, Tom saw another agent at the far end of the hall. His back was turned to them but not for long. The commotion in the kitchen had caught his attention and he was turning to investigate. In a split second Tom saw what looked like the only point of escape. To his left there was a door leading out onto what looked like a patio, so he charged in that direction. Shelly was reacting on blind instinct. Tom pulled and she moved. What she wasn't prepared for was being thrown through an open door. She went sprawling out onto the paving bricks, losing her microphone in the bushes. Tom was crouching against the door, low, beneath the window. He had his finger pressed hard against his lips, and she rolled into the bushes after her microphone.

Tom sniped toward her. She felt as if she were in a war zone from Alice in Wonderland. When he finally reached her, she couldn't restrain herself, "Are you crazy? We just got in the house, now we're outside again! I hope you have some brilliant plan up your sleeve!" She was annoyed, bruised and, although she couldn't see it, probably bleeding.

"Right now my brilliant plan is to stay alive and free!" Tom snapped back at her.

Shelly just wanted to stand up. Branches were poking through her clothing and the smell, which at one time seemed so beautiful, now just seemed putridly sweet. Tom seemed to be irritatingly masculine with all his ducking, hiding and shoving. He had always been so laid back and nonchalant. Where did all this behavior come from?

Snapping her attention back to their present situation, Tom punched her arm slightly, drawing her focus to a pair of French doors. Standing around a cart laden with liquor, were the five gentlemen of interest.

"We've got to get closer." Tom whispered. "If we crawl to the bench we'll be able to get a good picture. A little closer and maybe we'll get a little sound."

"I'm not to sure I can crawl anywhere! Tom, maybe we're in over our heads?" Shelly, not normally one to admit defeat, was genuinely scared. What had started out as an exciting adventure was becoming dangerous and even a little too real for her.

Recognizing fear in her voice, Tom was a little irritated. What had she expected this was going to be, a cakewalk?

"We can't stop now! You can do it. It's just a little ways to the bench. You stick with the camera and I'll get closer to the door. I know we'll get some sound. If we're going to get out of this we might as well get out with something, right?"

Tom made sense. It was an all or nothing situation. "Sure, you're right. I'm a smaller target. I'll roll up to the doors. You stay with the camera." Shelly's pluck was coming back.

Giving her a ready, set, go look they crawled to the bench. Tom started shooting immediately while Shelly took a deep breath and did a slow roll toward the sidewall. The men inside were to intent on what Marcus Holland was saying to notice anything outside the doors. Shelly stretched her arm as far as she could. What were the chances that the door would be ajar? *Someone must really be looking out for us*, was her only thought. Suddenly, out of nowhere came the phrase, "He shall give his angels charge over you to keep thee."

Mr. Holland seemed to be playing to a captive audience. Although they all seemed to be there voluntarily, there also seemed to be something very involuntary about them. They were acting almost by rote rather than by reason. "I assume all the layoffs will begin on schedule?"

A collective murmur of affirmation came from the group.

"Good. I think you will all be pleased with your bonuses. Our plans are moving ahead nicely. As soon as some of our more prominent senators and congressmen see things more clearly, your jobs should be a little easier, without as many questions."

"Mr. Holland, your car is waiting." The Secret Service agent from the hallway announced. In an instant Shelly froze. Fortunately for her, his interest was only in getting the Vice President out of the building safely.

"I hope you gentlemen will enjoy your lunch. I'm sorry that I can't stay but there is much to do."

Once Mr. Holland left the room, Shelly rolled slowly back to the bench.

"Let's get out of here!" Heading back toward the bushes, there was a slight fall to the ground just beyond them. As they hit the ground, Tom and Shelly heard the commotion.

"Where did those two reporters go?" The agents they had run into earlier were scanning the grounds for them.

"The last time I saw them, they were under the trees over there. They've got to be here, their van is still parked on the road." Moving quickly toward the trees, the agents were like bloodhounds on a scent.

From the cover of their bushes, Tom and Shelly burst back into the building and then through the kitchen entrance knocking the chef to the floor. Knowing what awaited them outside, both stopped abruptly by the door they entered into so secretly minutes before. Now they were almost directly across from the van.

"We'll have to make an all out run for the van. You ready?"

Shelly just nodded. Bolting from beneath the bushes it seemed that they were in the clear. Then the shouting rang out.

"Hey! You over there, halt or we will shoot!"

Thank heavens Tom never remembered to close the side van door. Tom dove into the door with Shelly hot on his heels. Before she could reach behind her to slam the door shut, Tom had the van started and was screeching away. No shots had rung out and Shelly lay on the floor of the van heaving her lungs out.

Shelly was scared but excited at the same time. Her heart was pounding in her ears and there wasn't enough air to breathe. Never had she had to go to such lengths to get her story.

Before he could pull the trigger, his partner yanked his arm. "What are you doing?" Rage was evident in his voice. "I had a clear shot!"

"Yeah, and what were we going to tell the press, the cops and everyone else with two dead reporters on the grounds?" Annoyance was the mood of the day. Working with gun happy junior agents was such a delight. "Don't get your undies in a twist. I got the license number of the van, not to mention the three foot letters 'BBS . . . stories you can count on' on the van."

CHAPTER 11

"Pastor Hayes, it's been months since we started the park vigil. Has anything happened? I mean, with all respect, I really thought that we would have seen something by now!" Clint was agitated and clearly impatient.

"Clint, God works in His time." replied Pastor Hayes.

"I understand that. Unfortunately, I'm going broke trying to feed all the people who are coming in needing groceries. The food pantries can't keep up with the demand. The welfare services are drying up and I feel like I'm stuck in the middle."

Pastor Hayes could read the stress on Clint's face. It wasn't easy trying to keep people inspired to do the right thing. With God it isn't always easy to see the light at the end of the tunnel. He just couldn't find any new words of encouragement for Clint.

"Mary! I'm so glad to see you again!" Pastor sighed in relief, as Mary entered the room. "Clint I know things are difficult right now, but it's that way for everyone. We need to stay strong. We are a witness for Christ!" His words sounded weak even to himself. "Why don't we sit down? I wanted to thank you for the great job you're doing with the youth group! It's not easy keeping momentum going when the results aren't evident."

Clint squirmed a little in his chair. People always want miracles without sacrifice or pain. Hadn't he just been complaining about the same thing himself?

"I heard Esther and the group ran across a young reporter that stopped and talked with them. What was happening with that?"

"Well, according to Esther, she was there to get a human interest story and ended up talking about her own experiences. To me it sounded like she knows something about the Holy Ghost. It's kind of exciting. I guess Esther's going to be talking with her again. I think she may have gotten the Holy Spirit as a child."

"So young she just doesn't remember?" asked Pastor Hayes.

"Pastor we did invite her to church, but as of yet we haven't seen her. I believe she worked for BBS."

"That's fine. Clint, it looks to me like God is doing something. *She may be the start of something big. Any soul won for God is something big!*"

Clint felt a glimmer of renewal. Pastor was right. God was starting the work. Clint was missing it because he was looking for "big" things. The journey of a thousand steps starts with the first one. Clint silently chided himself.

"Mary, we need to relieve Esther at the store. It's stressful there, and I'm sure she could use a break."

Mary stopped for a moment remembering a phone call she received earlier in the day. "Clint, do you remember Esther's friend from collage? Her name is Ruth."

"What about her?"

"Ruth's boyfriend has disappeared." "Fred? When? How?" Clint's response was one out of great concern. "Calm yourself Clint. I know whom you're talking about." replied Pastor Hayes. "I believe his name is Fred Joiner. He was the one who helped Esther at the park, wasn't he?"

Mary nervously held Clint's hand "Yes Pastor. Ruth is asking if we could keep an eye out for him also for prayer." The three joined hands immediately and began to pray. All three recognized the darkness out there and it wasn't getting better; at least not yet.

Fred Joiner was making quite a name for himself. He had become President McChellan's personal secretary.

"I'm so glad you decided to join us, Fred! You know, Marcus spoke highly of you! It's good to have friends you know and that you can trust around you. Don't you agree?"

"Yes, sir." Fred replied. It had been strange the night Fred came to visit Marcus. They had that argument at campaign headquarters. Fred really had not expected to talk to Marcus again. Things seemed a little hazy from then on. He remembered being cross with Marcus but when McChellan shook his hand all his anger seemed to have dissipated.

Fred never was quite sure what happened after that except that he had been offered the position of personal secretary to the President, which he accepted almost by command.

President McChellan handed Fred a list of names that consisted of both senators and well known business executives. "Fred, please call these people and let them know I wish to see them. Oh, and Fred, don't take no for an answer!"

At the top of the list were Senators Ben Cross and Marge McCurry. What was unusual about these first two names was that they were usually the two major senators that would go up against most of the President's policies on capital hill. The next two names were the executives of the top motor companies in America, Jack Mason, and Nasaki Yuhma. The most impressive name of all was at the bottom of the list, Frank B. Ashford, President of Ashford Investments, the largest investment firm on Wall Street.

Senator Cross had to be won over or brought to the same type of understanding. He wielded a strong influence over the senate. With him on McChellan's side it would be easy to push through his plans for the future.

"Senator Cross, I'm so glad that you could find the time to talk with me." Ever the gentlemen, McChellan's charm oozed out like too much frosting between cookies. Senator Cross was not impressed. It was his charisma that got him elected in the first place, certainly not his policies. "Please, have a seat."

NEIL FREISCHMIDT

"I'm always glad to receive an invitation from the Oval Office." Cross wasn't immune to using charm. "I would imagine that you are very busy, suppose we come to the point immediately."

"Ah, Senator Cross, you are a man after my own heart. As you are well aware, you have quite a bit of influence over the senate. I could use that influence on my side." There was an eerie tone to McChellan's voice and an even creepier look in his eye.

"Well, Mr. President, you would have that support if I could agree with your plans." Senator Cross just wanted this interview to end and be on his way.

"Actually, we really aren't that far apart on the issues. I think it is just our general approach to the solution!"

"I really don't see any compromise in the future. Unless, of course, you were to change your position on the economy and how to fix it."

"Well, I can see that we will need a little more time than we have now to discuss this. Perhaps we could have dinner sometime in the near future?" McChellan offered his hand in friendship. Relieved that this was the end of the conversation, Senator Cross firmly grasped the offered hand. As their hands met, a dark wisp moved over Cross' hand. Creeping up his arm, it seemed to penetrate Senator Cross' thoughts. Feeling slightly light-headed he couldn't imagine just what it was that he had objected to about President McChellan's plans.

"I'm sure we'll be able to work together to achieve our objectives."

"Yes." This was the only answer that seemed to come to mind. As Senator Cross closed the door behind him, again the slow smile of conquest spread over McChellan's face.

"Fred! Show the other gentlemen in, please!" McChellan stood at the doorway ready to welcome his new conquests still feeling the power from his last victory. After twenty minutes the door opened "Please, gentlemen, remember that time is short. Your immediate attention is required!" The men, looking vacant, just nodded in compliance.

"Fred, please come in for a minute. I have something special for you to do."

Lying down on his leather couch, McChellan placed his arms over his forehead as if deep in thought.

"Fred . . . ." Before he could finish his question Fred foolishly interrupted him "Sir, I was just on my way to remind you." Before he could begin his next word McChellan sat up angrily.

"Those young people that are camping in the park, do you know any of them?"

Stumbling to find the right words, "*Yes*." was all that come out,

"I'm afraid those young people are causing me a great deal of concern. It is my understanding that they are '*praying*'. They, of course, have every right to '*pray*,' however, it is starting to annoy me."

"Vice President Holland seems to think you may know one of these diligent young people. As a precautionary measure, I have had pictures taken of the various groups. There seems to be a leader among the pack and it's this young lady."

Handing Fred the picture, McChellan saw the flicker of recognition in Fred's eyes. It was a picture of Esther.

"Do you know her?"

"Yes, sir, I do."

"Good, I want her investigated. Maybe you can do that for me? I know how thorough you are. I'm relying on you to get me all the information on her."

"Yes, sir, right away."

"It is good to have people I trust working with me. By the way, what was it you were going to say?"

"I just wanted to remind you that the senate floor opens in just a few minutes."

At times his curiosity got the better of him. McChellan wanted to see how his new staff would obey his instructions. Since all senate floor proceedings could be monitored from his office, he decided to let his next meeting wait while he watched for himself.

"Turn on the set, Fred, I wish to watch."

"The House is now in session." A white haired, elderly woman appeared at the podium.

"Senator Agnes Whiting will now lead us in the Pledge of Allegiance."

Looking over the crowd, she raised her hand with pride.

"I pledge allegiance to the flag of the United States of America and to the Republic for which it stands, one nation with liberty and justice for all."

Rising from his seat, Senator William Morrison, cleared his throat.

"I would like to thank Senator Whiting for leading us in the Pledge. With all due respect, I would like to point out that you misspoke! *You forgot 'under God'.*"

"The gentleman from Texas is very observant! I didn't forget, *I just chose not to say it.*" Her reply was cool and calculated.

"I don't recall having taken a vote to change the Pledge, which has been said in these hallowed halls since the first assembly of this body. We have been giving God thanks from the very beginning. Who do you think you are?"

"I'm an American!" she responded coldly. "Now sit down!" Her voice was high and shrill. Senator Morrison looked out over the floor. Out of frustration he picked up his paperwork and headed toward the chamber door. Glancing over his shoulder, he was pleased to see a handful of other Senators following in the same direction.

Regaining the composure that she had obviously lost, Senator Whiting continued, "I'd like to offer up a bill that the President and I feel will be in the best interest of the American people!"

Morrison turned abruptly, bristling at her every word, and interrupted, "Before we begin new business, answer me this Senator. Do you believe in God Senator?" Once again the slow lazy drawl sounded throughout the chamber.

"Senator Morrison, I thought you left!" The shock in her voice drew a chuckle from the floor. "The question should be should anyone who doesn't believe in God have to read His name while reciting our country's pledge? I stand before you to introduce a new bill aiming to help all Americans, not just people who believe in God! The bill is titled *'Freedom from Prejudice Act'*. It covers all forms of prejudice and makes it a federal crime to discriminate against those that don't fit into the conventional and restrictive guidelines of traditional thought. There is no such thing as sticks and stones anymore! Inflammatory words and restrictive thinking are destroying this country. It is time that this situation is dealt with swiftly and severely! It had to be done in our schools so hiding behind the guise of a church or antiqued teachings of intolerance in homes would not be suffered!"

A loud round of applause rang throughout the chamber. Her indignation and eloquence of speech had done its duty. In disbelief Senator Morrison watched as man after man stood to honor these ridiculous words. The vote was called for. *'Yeas'* rang out across the room. As if he were in another dimension, he heard the gavel being brought down. The bill had been passed! There had been no discussion, no questions. It had been accepted like an infant accepts a spoon of peas from its mother.

"Mr. Speaker!" Senator Morrison's voice was incredulous, "has this bill gone through all the proper channels? None of us have heard of it until just now! A vote can't be taken. The bill can't be ratified. There are parliamentary procedures that need to be followed!"

"I believe it is too late for that!" The Senators face was twisted into an evil grimace. She was flush with victory. President McChellan will be very pleased with today's work.

The chamber came to a complete silence. Morrison knew that continuing was futile. He turned in utter disbelief and walked numbly toward the chamber doors. Something was terribly wrong here.

Problems were arising all over the nation. Large industries from each end of the country began to close and layoffs were now at an all time high. One industry, however, was still producing and that company was Aztec motors. However, the question was for how long?

Sitting quietly at her desk, senior accountant for Aztec Motors, Fran Staples was going over the numbers from the week's sales. In one week, the company nearly doubled the sales they had last year.

"Hey, Fran, are you going to the meeting?" *That rough voice,* she thought to herself, *could only be one person, Jim Carpenter.* Peeking around the corner of her cubical, a balding, heavy-set man sat spinning in his chair as if he was still in his childhood.

"What meeting, Jim?"

"Gee! Fran, don't you ever read your e-mails?"

"Awe, Jim, you know I don't have time for stuff like that!" Opening her e-mail file she noticed multiple e-mails from various departments each containing the usual stuff, bring donuts for someone's birthday, policies on sexual harassment, policies against smoking, etc., whatever!

Poking his head around the side of the cubical, Jeff just gave his big, stupid, country boy grin, "See the one about the mandatory meeting? Must be something big. Guess who came through those doors an hour ago?"

Now he had her attention. Jim was always good for juicy gossip and, usually, he was pretty reliable. "Who?"

"Jack Mason!"

"Get out! He's never made an appearance here before. Why is the head of Aztec coming here? Why did he show up now?"

"Don't know, but we better get a move on. The higher ups are all doing a spring mating dance and don't want anyone coming in late!"

Fran and Jim began the long walk down the hall toward the cafeteria. What a place to hold a meeting with Jack Mason. They must really want to shove a load of garbage down our throats, trying to be so down to earth and homey! Fran had a bad feeling about this one.

The room was packed. She was surprised that the janitors hadn't been invited. Heck even the mailman wouldn't have surprised her. By the expressions on everyone's face, you would have thought someone died.

She reached over, took Jim's hand, and moved over to the seating area.

"Careful, honey, this could be sexual harassment!" Jim grinned. He could feel the tension as well.

Head tables were set up in the front of the vending machines. Of course, they were on risers. It was a subtle way of letting everyone know that they were in charge. Up on the platform were all of the top executives of the D.C. plant, including Jack Mason. Their faces held little or no expression at all. Usually, she thought, their faces give it away, but not this time. She noticed Alice Keys, the company president's assistant secretary, wiping away tears from her eyes.

"That's not good!" Jim whispered as he nudged her arm.

"No, it's not, Jim." she whispered back.

"Hey, guys, do you have any idea what this is about?" Jim and Fran turned around. Clarence Banks and the other production managers sat looking very apprehensive. Smiling, Fran replied "No, sorry!"

"Ladies and gentlemen, please be seated. It is my pleasure to introduce to you the President and CEO of Aztec Motors, Mr. Jack Mason!" A tentative applause broke out.

"Thank you very much." Jack Mason stood looking like an executioner. "As you all are well aware, our country is facing difficult economic times. Our sales are down, way down, from previous years. Our company is losing money in every department including parts and service. Union workers are up for a new contract soon, and we really don't know how that will work out. Beginning next month, 120 workers from the D.C. plant will be put on permanent layoff."

A loud murmur moved through the room. It was exactly as everyone had feared. Fran turned to Jim but it wasn't with fear, it was with confusion. She had just seen the sales figures for the month. They were double the sales figures for the whole of last year!

"We at Aztec Motors are concerned about you and your families! A generous severance package will be given, along with a promise of help with education through federally funded programs, should you desire that direction. Thank you".

Jack Mason gathered his papers and prepared to leave the room.

Before Fran knew what she was doing, she had literally jumped up from her chair.

"Wait a minute, Mr. Mason. My name is Fran Staples. I'm an accountant here."

Jack Mason's neck nearly snapped as his head turn sharply to look at her. "I'm sorry, Ms. Staples, but we really don't have time for a question and answer period. All questions should be directed to your immediate supervisors." His tone was cold and very final. The door had been firmly slammed in her face.

Angrily, Fran snatched Jim's sleeve. She nearly pulled him off his chair as she snarled, "They're not going to get away with this! We're not going down that easy!"

She knew they made money last year! She handled all the paperwork. She knew the numbers, but she needed proof! Dragging Jim behind her, she made for her computer. All the proof she needed would be there in the spreadsheets.

"Whoa, Bessie! I'd like to use this arm after work tonight." Jim extracted his sleeve from her vice-like grip.

"All the proof I need is on my computer. Aztec made a ton of money last month! That whole speech was a load of manure! Look, here it is. Fran's fingers flew over the keys, typing in her password. With a flourish she hit the enter button. Nothing happened. The screen was black. "What's going on?"

"You must have typed wrong. Just calm down a little and type it in again." Jim was catching her agitation.

"I'm locked out of my computer!"

Now Jim was beginning to see the picture that Fran had seen all along.

"Let me try mine. It could just be a glitch. You know how finicky these hunks of junk are."

After several tries, he was unsuccessful. In the short time since the end of the meeting and the walk back to their workstations, all access to computers had been shut down.

"So they want to play hardball!" she exclaimed. Glancing up at Jim. "I've got it! Clarence's office is across the street! If I can get to his computer I can access my files!"

Across the street, Clarence sat at his desk in shock. He had been with the company for 20 years, all his hard work, and now this.

He thought the company was on the upswing! After all the overtime they had been putting in to make extra parts. He didn't understand. What would his wife think? He couldn't take early retirement at least not this early in his life, and not after the hit their 401K had taken. It all seemed so hopeless.

"Clarence, please let me use your computer! It's very important!" Fran and Jim were out of breath from their frantic run across the street.

"Why? What's wrong with your computer?" Was everyone going mad?

"I don't have time, just log in and let me use your computer!" Seeing the distressed look on Clarence's face had a calming effect on both Fran and Jim.

"Look Clarence, something is hinky. The company isn't telling the truth and Fran here knows it. Unfortunately, they've locked us out of our computers. We're in an awful big hurry, so what do you say?" Jim could charm the skin off a snake when he needed to!

"Well, I suppose. You're not doing anything illegal? I mean, it is my login and you know how protective they are about that stuff." Clarence wasn't sure but, on the other hand, in some small way he felt like he was getting revenge on the company that just knifed him in the back.

"No! I just need to print a report or two for backup purposes!" Fran wasn't a good liar but it seemed like a good way to protect Clarence. Smiling, Fran leaned down and gave him a slight peck on the cheek, and whispered "Thank you!"

As soon as Clarence logged in and left the office, Fran leapt into action. "Sure enough, I knew it!" she whispered. As fast as the computer could download she transferred the reports onto her u-disk.

"Why Fran, Jim, what are you doing here? What would accounting need in engineering?"

It was Alice Keyes, head of personnel.

"Well," Fran started but couldn't think of anything but the blinking light on the u-disk. It kept announcing, "'hey look at me'!'

Jim also saw the light, but unlike Fran was a little quicker with an explanation. "The news of the company's down turn was so shocking! We've known Clarence for a long time and were a little worried about how he was taking the news." The lie rolled off his lips like honey dripping off a spoon. Fran wondered just how much lying Jim had done in the past.

"Where is Clarence?" Alice eyed both of them with suspicion. "I know that he understands the rules about leaving his workstation with his computer left on. I think we all know that rule!"

If Jim just moved a little to his left, Fran would be able to punch the sleep button without Alice seeing her. Thank heavens Clarence was distraught! On the corner of the desk was a cup of coffee, another infraction of the rules. Inching her hand forward, Fran pinged the cup just hard enough to send its contents spilling down Jim's right pant leg.

"Ow!" The steamy coffee soaked Jim's pants and sent him jumping to the left. As soon as he jumped, Fran grabbed the disk from its port. Alice had been temporarily distracted but not temporarily enough.

"What's that?" she demanded. Timidly, Fran stood.

"Oh, this?" She tried to wave the disk nonchalantly in the air. "Clarence and I sometimes play computer games at lunch. I thought that if I brought one over, it might calm his nerves. You know, a little buddy therapy?"

Jim couldn't help but think how inept Fran was at lying. She couldn't pull the wool over anyone's eyes even if *they* handed her the blanket.

Putting the disc back in her pocket, Fran looked at Alice nervously. "This happens to be mine." she said with a weak smile.

Alice Keys just kept staring at her intently! "Games, huh." Her voice was flat sounding. How big of a fool did these two think she was? There were a lot of games being played this morning! The question was, who was going to be on the winning side?

"That's right games!" Fran saw the slightest glimmer of indecision in Alice's eyes.

Alice Keys' shoulders just dropped. The sternness on her face was replaced with a resolute grimace. "I don't know too much about what games are what. Don't have much time for them or interest. Seems some can get you in a lot of trouble if they aren't played right."

Fran, knowing Alice was no dummy, just smiled, "Thank you, Alice!"

Fighting the urge to turn and bolt, Jim and Fran walked slowly back to their department, knowing what would happen if they had been caught!

CHAPTER 12

On the other side of town evil began the second step in the fight.

"Hello! Is anyone here?"

"Be right there!" Esther had been taking inventory in the back room. There had been so many "*free*" groceries given out because of the times, the inventory had been neglected. Putting down her paperwork, Esther headed in the direction of the voice. "I'm sorry, I was finishing up some last minute inventory! Now, how can I help you?"

"You could give an old friend the time of day." Fred stood with his hands on his hips.

"Oh my gosh! Fred!" She was tongue-tied! Everything she tried to say came out twisted and wrong. She threw her arms around Fred's neck. It was good to see him. Although Fred returned her hug, it didn't seem as warm as the hugs of old. There was a coolness present that had never been there before but, then, they hadn't seen or talked to each other for quite some time. "Hey! Just where have you been! Ruth and I have been missing you! One day you were there and then you were gone! I never did get to thank you for going down and trying to talk to Marcus for me. I really don't know what happened."

"Yes, well, you're welcome. You know, it was all for the best. Marcus is a very busy man and doesn't have much time for a social life." Fred seemed oddly cold and defensive where Marcus was concerned.

Getting some coffee, the two sat down to make up for lost time.

"I've been doing some traveling." Fred offered.

"Why didn't you at least contact us and let us know where you were? A postcard would have been nice." Esther was trying to get back some of that old feeling between them. Their conversation was beginning to feel forced.

"Because I wanted to find myself."

"I didn't know you were lost!"

"I don't expect you to understand, but I felt I needed to sever all ties to my old life, even if it meant hurting some of the people I loved." The words sounded good, but they just didn't match the feeling Esther was getting from Fred. "I'm sorry if I hurt you."

Just for an instant there was a glimmer of the old Fred that Esther knew. It was gone as quickly as it came, as Fred continued, "I need a job, something to get a little money in my pocket before I leave again."

Esther was bewildered as to why Fred stopped by if he only meant to leave again. "I'll keep my ears open. If I hear of something, I'll let you know, that is, if you leave me a phone number."

"Yes." Fred reached into his pocket and pulled out a plain looking business card. It only had his name on it and a phone number. Nothing more. Handing it to her, "Call me anytime. I'm usually just hanging around. I'd better be going. Have some errands to do." He gave Esther a peck on the cheek and left as quietly as he had arrived.

Something just didn't seem to add up. Fred was Fred but he wasn't. He was traveling around but he had a phone number where he could be reached any time. He had no job but he still had a business card. He needed money but he was freshly shaved and sheared. His suit was pressed, of good quality and he smelled of soap and cologne, expensive cologne. Things didn't make sense.

CHAPTER 13

Pacing back and forth in his office, Senator Thomas Peeling, was going over the speech that he and Senator Morrison had put together. Their plan included more tax cuts aimed at helping small businesses and to give incentives to larger companies to stop moving their production overseas as a way of escaping the huge tax levies placed on them by the McChellan administration.

"Senator Peeling, I'm sorry to interrupt you, but have you seen this?" His aide was holding a stack of pages the size of four Washington telephone directories. Walking over to the stack of papers, Peeling read the top page. It was an $800 trillion dollar stimulus bill sponsored by President McChellan.

"When did you get this?"

"Just a few minutes ago, sir. Everyone is just now receiving their copy."

"I guess I'll need to read all this." The resignation in his voice was disheartening.

"You had better hurry!" responded his aide.

"Why, what's the big hurry?"

Hesitantly, knowing how Peeling was going to react, he offered quietly, "Sir, this bill is being introduced today. There's talk about certain senators wanting to pass it through right away."

"How can they expect to do that? Get Senator Morrison on the phone! Now!"

Angrily, Peeling began reading the top half of the bill.

"How can they expect me to vote for something I haven't even had a chance to read? $800 trillion dollars! For what?" This was happening way too fast. The Senator's mind was reeling at a hundred miles an hour. Reading the bill, he was beginning to think there was a conspiracy within the government. Conspiracy against the American people and, if this was true, just how far did it go? Worry spread through him as if ice water had just been poured through his veins.

"Peeling!" A loud powerful voice shouted from his door. Startled, Peeling turned. It was Ben Cross, standing in his usual strong stature.

"Talking to yourself again, Peeling?" He asked with his usual smug expression. Senator Peeling snapped out of his daze and quickly turned. Ben Cross was not a man to be fooled with. With him everything was neat and trim and in it's place. He was a senators' senator, if you didn't mind crocodiles on a leash. Some compared him to a master sergeant in the Marine Corps.

Peeling froze. He stood embarrassed with his shirttails hanging out. Old pizza boxes and soda cans were cluttering his office as if he were a dorm student in college rather than a senator. Trying to muster up some form of dignity, he steadied his gaze directly at the intruder.

"Senator, have you seen this?"

"As a matter of fact, I have. I've read it." he replied smiling.

"But how? I have just received my copy a few minutes ago!"

"That's too bad. We thought that by now everyone should have had a chance to read it. It was sent out three weeks ago."

Peeling leaned against his desk confused.

"Senator Cross, I need more time."

"Now, Peeling, of course, I understand how you must feel. It isn't easy keeping up with the work load here in Washington and still getting in a social life." He glanced about the office with barely veiled disgust.

Now all embarrassment was gone. It was replaced with a mixture of anger and outrage. Peeling knew Ben Cross and Ben Cross knew Peeling. Ben knew that Peeling didn't waste his time chasing the more than available skirts in town nor did he waste his time with idle tomfoolery. The fact that this attitude was coming from Ben confused him.

"Peeling, you were given three weeks to read the bill. Can we expect your support?"

Peeling, no longer intimated by Senator Cross, slammed his hand down on the bill.

"Ben," he replied sharply, "I just received it today! No matter what you might think, I cannot, in all good conscience, vote for this bill, this soon!"

Ben Cross, looking disappointed at this young Senator, began his famous slow walk, the one he used to intimidate people. There was something about his demeanor, that large belly and baggy pants. His face would change from a warm smile to eyes that looked hurt while at the same time seemed to penetrate your soul causing you to feel guilty about letting him down. He usually got his way. Not turning to look at the young senator, "Peeling, son," his tone was fatherly, "I know this bill is right for America and the American people. Just look at what's happening out there! Wall Street is broke! Our economy needs a boost, and this bill will provide that!"

Looking sternly at Peeling, his tone no longer fatherly, but forceful, "The President believes in this bill, and so do I. That should be enough for you to believe in it too, don't you think?"

Peeling, knowing when to shut up, just sat down angrily. Believing that he had accomplished his task, Ben Cross leisurely took his leave. Peeling felt like he just lived through a hurricane in a tree house.

Senator Peeling began to look over the bill once more. A man of Ben Crosses' reputation agreeing to such a thing! This was not the usual Ben Cross.

The entire office floor was in a state of confusion. The sound of footsteps raced past Senator Morrison's door. Senator Morrison sat in his office attempting to page through a huge bill that was just placed before him.

"$800 trillion?" he blurted out angrily! "What the heck for!"

"Sir," his aide had walked into his office, delivering a much-needed cup of coffee, "Senator Peeling on line two, and there's a women here to see you! She doesn't have an appointment but she says it is very urgent." Frustration filled Morrison. What is going on around here? Bills began showing up out of nowhere. People were showing up needing to be seen without appointments. Morrison was an organized man. He didn't take kindly to having things shoved on him without preparation.

"Please ask her to wait. I need to talk to Senator Peeling first." Maybe Peeling knew more about this so called stimulus bill.

"Peeling, what's going on?"

"Ben Cross paid me a visit!"

Morrison, resting his head on his hand, "Ben? What did he want?"

Peeling told him of their conversation and how he tried to intimidate him into voting for his side.

"Peeling we have a few hours before session. Let's meet for lunch. I only live a few blocks from here, say in about forty minutes. I'll pick up lunch for us both on my way down. I have an appointment now. But after that I'll be free."

Hanging up, Morrison wet a handkerchief and placed it over his tired eyes. The last thing he wanted to do was to meet with a woman about who knows what. It was either going to be some lengthy discussion about something important or a frivolous waste of time talking about the colors for a party of some kind. Either way, he just didn't have the time or the attention span for either.

"Maybe I can be of help!" A soft and friendly voice came from across the room. Slowly he lowered the cloth from his eyes. A middle-aged woman stood at the door of his office. Morrison was taken. His eyes moved up and down the figure that approached him. Her bright blue dress fit her frame well, and the way she moved swayed with a touch of grace. Suddenly he didn't feel quite so tired. "I'm sorry, but your secretary stepped away from his desk and I heard you hang up the phone. I hope you don't mind my walking in like this?"

Straightening his tie and running his hand through his hair, Morrison was finding it hard to find words. He was annoyed that she had just walked in but then on the other hand he was glad she did.

"Not at all. Can I help you?" His voice came out sounding high and squeaky, making him blush with embarrassment.

"I believe I can help you, Senator."

Walking over to a set of chairs standing along the wall, he pulled his favorite leather chair up to his desk. "Please have a seat, Ms . . . I'm sorry I didn't catch your name."

"My name is Jill Rafferty. I'm sorry to say that I helped create this mess."

"What mess and how did you do it?" He replied jokingly.

"Senator Morrison, I think you know what mess I'm referring to." Jill glanced at the bill on his desk. "I came to you because I know that you're not with the ones involved with this situation."

Morrison stopped for a moment just looking at the woman, who, just a few minutes ago made him feel like a school boy. Now all he could think of was what a fool he was for allowing her in his office.

This knock out just comes out of the blue and adds even more mystery to all the other peculiar activities going on, this was all he needed. Trying to pretend not to know what she was referring too he decided to play along to see where this went. "O.K tell me about what's going on?"

She looked at him coldly; knowing he was playing ignorant with her caused her to feel uneasy. She stopped for a moment and considered leaving, perhaps just staying out of the whole mess.

She knew the importance of what she had to offer; all the while looking at Morrison deciding if he was the right man to bring this to. She was no ones' fool and didn't like being treated like one.

"I helped President McChellan get into the Whitehouse "she said sadly." His eyes grew wide, "I recognize you now! You were his campaign manager, weren't you!" "Senator Morrison, I believe their goal is for total government take over."

"Ms Rafferity the government is in charge" he responded skeptically. Hesitantly, she began explaining what she had seen the day of the President's acceptance speech but stopped short of discussing the black shadow creatures knowing he wouldn't understand.

This discussion was difficult to begin with, but telling about shadow creatures would have had her removed from his office. She knew that there were forces at work here that went beyond normal, but the expression on the senator's face told her that now was not the time to try and explain super natural phenomena.

She decided to put it in terms he would understand.

"No you don't understand, I'm talking socialism, communism. Absolute power!"

Morrison looked at her sternly. What she was saying was crazy! He was having problems believing anything she was saying. However, he couldn't deny that what she was saying did seem to fit all the weird happenings around the senate.

Feeling slighted and angered, Jill stood to her feet and placed both hands on his desk. She looked him straight in his eyes,

"Senator Morrison! Is everyone in the senate blind? Don't you think that it's weird that all the auto industries went broke at the same time? Her demeanor began to change as she spoke.

"How about the paper companies in the north? Why did they suddenly begin to lose money worldwide? Doesn't anyone here on Capital hill see through these things? And what about Wall Street? I can't believe anyone in congress isn't suspicious!"

"Stop!" He blurted out loudly. Suspicious of what?"

"What do you think really happened to all those stocks and bonds that suddenly disappeared from all the retirement accounts? Do you really believe all that money just disappeared?"

"Ms. Rafferity, it was investigated thoroughly by the FBI."

Jill knew this was going to be tough convincing the Senator on what she knew. Arguing would get her nowhere, so she stopped pushing her point and lowered her tone of voice.

"No, Senator, they didn't! It's all an illusion! I have documents here proving that orders were given by the director himself to over look certain investigations. No money went anywhere! Instead, they are making the American people believe it happened that way!"

"How can I believe any of this? he responded. You are talking about the heads of the top FBI units under the President. Some of them happen to be good friends of mine!" She knew she had to try something that would require a little faith in her theory, something that would penetrate that thick head of his.

"Listen to me Senator. When you hear that President McChellan uses his authoritative powers to activate the Emergency Directive Act and instructs state governments to direct all foreclosure accounts to be managed by one bank, namely, the United States Bank, you will know that I'm telling the truth. Once the bill, the one that you're holding in your hands, gets passed, this government will have control over all the financial and industrial markets throughout the United States!"

"Senator that bill is worded so that all money given out will be considered a loan, making those institutions that except the monies answerable to the government."

Morrison sat back stunned, "Why the scheme about Wall Street?"

"In order to have a bill like the stimulus package succeed, they need to create fear. A type of fear that would cause the people to turn toward the government for help. They knew the people wouldn't be so reluctant to pass a bill of such magnitude if the people actually felt the need for it. 800 trillion is a lot of money. Getting their retirement money back seems more important then the higher taxes that will be required to pay for it. However, they are blinded to the administration's real objective. Total government control. Senator! Remember, it's the same CEO's who ran the businesses into the ground that will profit from this stimulus package. You will find that each of those people received large amounts of money, in the sum of $30 million. They just called them bonuses." Morrison began to be convinced.

"Yes, I do remember something about that. I had many people call and complain,"

"Senator Morrison how could all these failing business afford to give out $30 million dollars in bonuses to each of their CEO's?"

"Do you have proof? I mean something concrete! Something we can take to the people. We are out numbered on the floor and probably won't be able to stop this thing from happening." He said somberly.

"Tell me one thing, Ms Rafferity, how did they get all the firms from Wall Street to go along with this?"

"Senator, they took enough funds from the pension fund, 401 accounts, IRAs' and stocks to raise questions within the firms. Then they used the media to bring it to the people creating fear, causing them to run to their respective brokers and insist on their money, which, in most cases; was already made invisible. That's how all those CEO's received their money! So, if the FBI truly wants to find the money, have them investigate all the CEO's. Sadly, think of all those poor, innocent people sitting in prison who took the blame for all those missing pensions."

Everything she just said seemed to fit. He couldn't go to the FBI with a "because I said so!" That just wasn't going to wash. If it was true that a cover up took place, who would listen? Friends or not, this had to be brought out.

"Do you have anything on paper?"

"I have these that I can give you now." With that she handed over to Morrison a medium sized envelope about one inch thick containing documents and pictures. She informed him that the documents were obtained from the Whitehouse from people she knew and trusted who still worked within this administration.

"I know that I can get more, but it will be difficult and dangerous. I'll try and get whatever paper work I can. In the mean time contact Shelly Cleveland from BBS news. There's a pastor from a small church in town that seems to have a lot of information on this. His name is Pastor Nathanial Hayes. He pastors at Christ's Sword United Pentecostal Church. I already placed a tip with them in the past. For some reason, they seem to have a great deal of knowledge concerning this matter. Ms. Cleveland, I understand, being a reporter, but the Pastor? I still don't understand why he's involved. I hear they are having a meeting between all the different church denominations throughout the D.C. area. It may be in your interest to attend, Senator. Good luck sir."

CHAPTER 14

Later that afternoon Morrison arrived home trying to at least be somewhat ready for his meeting with Senator Peeling. Senator Morrison noticed a large car parked at the end of the block. Inside the car two dark figures sat motionless.

"Don't they ever quit?" he asked himself. Reaching his doorway, he reached down and picked up his mail, *what's this?* Along with his usual mail was a large brown package. On the front of the package, *"For Senator Morrison's eyes only"* was written in large bold letters across the front of the cover. *Some times I feel like I'm living in a spy novel* he thought.

Once inside, he immediately knew something wasn't right. Furniture was moved and papers were out of place. Morrison quickly looked around for anything else that looked out of place. An uncomfortable feeling took hold in his stomach. Placing his mail down on the table he turned cautiously then walked slowly across his living room and removed a flashlight from the lower drawer of his desk.

Wait a minute! Where's Rex? Rex always welcomed him at the door! Walking faster through his home, he began calling for Rex hoping for a response but there was none causing Morrison great concern.

Morrison made his way up the stairs to the second floor, "Rex! Come on boy!" He whispers, but again no response. Stopping dead in his tracks, he stood and just listened. Nervously he became hopeful for Peeling's arrival. Another person in the house now would be most welcome.

Morrison slowly began walking down the hall listening for any sound that might lead him to his dog. Suddenly a well-placed hand covered his mouth, keeping Morrison from calling out. A strong arm wrapped around his waist pulling Morrison backwards causing him to lose his balance and fall hard against the wall. Breaking away from his assailant Morrison shoved his attacker back against a closet door causing the door to collapse.

"Bill! Wait! It's me!"

Morrison, preparing for a fight, glanced down to see Senator Peeling lying on the floor with two large closet doors on top of him. Morrison stunned, looked at him sternly.

"Peeling! Are you crazy? what are you doing?"

Crawling out from underneath the largest closet doors he had ever seen, Peeling began wiping away dirt and dust from his suit jacket. Holding up one finger to his lips, indicating to Morrison to keep quite, then he whispered into Morrison's ear, "The house is bugged!" Morrison stepped back looking at Peeling confused.

"How do you know this?"

"I found these three already. Heaven only knows how many more are around here." Taking hold of Morrison's arm, Peeling led him to the window. "There, in that car, they are listening to us."

"I saw them when I got home."

"The thing is, Bill, that they don't want us to get together for some reason. I found the same devices in my home. Oh, by the way, your dog is in your garage. It was the only way to keep him quiet."

"Alright you're here! Now what?" snapped Morrison. It was obvious that he didn't like all this espionage that was being forced on him!

"Do you have a place where we can talk?"

"Come on, we better get down stairs. I know a place."

The cellar was dark. Strangely the lights wouldn't turn on. Reaching up toward the ceiling Morrison pushed his hand up through a piece of ceiling tile and pushed a small button, opening a small door. "Come on in Peeling. It's my private place." he said, chuckling. The irony of him having a secret place suddenly struck him

Using two large cardboard boxes as seats, the two men sat and began discussing the events taking place within the house.

"Morrison do you have any idea on what's going on? I know they just passed that stimulus bill, but do you realize how many senators didn't have the chance to read the thing. The idea of $800 trillion! How do they expect to pay for it? Or, for that matter how can they explain this to the American taxpayer?"

Morrison looked somberly over at Peeling and began to share with him what took place in his office just a few hours before.

"Are you talking about the same Jill Rafferity that blew our socks off during the last election?

"Yep!" was all Morrison could say while sipping on his coffee. I guess she saw another side of her so-called hero. She gave me a package of papers and notes that were exchanged between Holland and McChellan, all of which describe in detail, all the people and places involved, and they all lead to directly to FBI involvement to this conspiracy!"

"That's a big word Bill, conspiracy. Have you read any of those papers?"

"Not yet, but I have them hidden, I guarantee that! So far I can prove payoffs to certain individuals in the FBI. The Wall Street thing is going to be the tough one. She did ask me to call someone from the BBS, a reporter named Cleveland. Rafferity claims to have provided a tip to her on an investigation she was working on."

"Bill, if we purse this and we are wrong . . . !"

"I don't believe that we are. Look at what's happening throughout the House and Congress. People are acting strange and bills are being passed illegally. I know you see it too. Thomas, I know we are not alone. Others from the hill have also contacted me and they are just as confused."

"No one wants to get involved! I wonder if I want to! Going against Ben Cross! He's one scary fellow!

"Well, Thomas, what do you suppose we do about this?"

"Bill, you know that election time is fast approaching. How would you feel about running for President of the United States?"

Morrison's eyes grew wide. "Something in that coffee,

Thomas?"

Peeling moved over and placed his arm around Morrison's shoulders as a sign of partnership. "Think about it. We haven't much in the way of support from our peers and we are out numbered in the house, but our side has yet to select a candidate to run against McChellan. If we go to our party and show them a plan, maybe we can get their endorsement."

"Thomas, how? I don't see it!"

"Now Bill, listen for a second. We need to find more proof I know it's out there!"

"All the major networks side with McChellan. Have you ever heard anything negative spoken about him through any of those stations?"

"That's why we go to BBS. You even said there's a reporter already investigating this thing, right? They also have been impartial."

Morrison shrugged his shoulders, seemingly more interested.

"O.K. Thomas. Let's do it, but this could mean the end to our careers!"

"If we don't, what happens to America?"

The two men sat silent for a moment, and then decided to end the meeting. "When we receive more information, keep it between us for now. We don't really know whom we can trust. Let's get on this fast. The faster we respond, the faster we can get it to the people!"

Shaking hands in agreement, they left the room making sure to close the door tightly behind them.

"Morrison, look!" Looking out the egress window, they saw dark shadows criss-crossing back and forth across the cellar window.

"It must be them!" whispered Morrison. "What now?"

Both men return to the hidden room to think of an escape plan for Peeling. Peeling remembered the old egress window on his grandparents' farm back in Wisconsin. He and his brothers used to play in the old cellar using the old tunnel as a means of escape and an attempt to elude his grandparents, especially toward bedtime. This gave him an idea.

Moving over to the large egress window, Peeling began lifting the heavy lid that lead to the outside. "Hey this worked at my grandpa's! Maybe it will work here too!"

Slowly they opened the window. "Looks good." whispered Morrison.

"No! Down!" whispered Peeling

Both men ducked down as fast as they could. Looking up, two large men dressed in black walked passed the window opening, followed by what seemed to be a long stream of black smoke. Both men looked around to see if anything was set on fire, but no fire alarms went off and no smell of burning was present. There was a strange color as they passed. It was sickeningly sweet and heavy. "What the heck was that?" asked Peeling. "This whole day has been strange why not the evening as well" replied Morrison. Once again all this dark smoke stuff was peculiar but, for now, all they wanted to do was escape.

The two men shook hands once more, and Peeling took off running through the neighbors yard. Morrison climbed back down, calmly latching the window.

On his way to the garage, to bring Rex into the house, Morrison passed by the table where he placed the package he had received in the mail. Curiosity got the best of him. He stopped and picked up the package, looking over the large brown envelope. He again read the large bold letters.

"*Just for my eyes hey!*"

He began unwrapping the brown paper covering tearing as fast as he could without ripping the contents. Silently he began to read the cover letter. Now even more confused then ever, he mumbled to himself "Who is Fran Staples?"

CHAPTER 15

Shelly and Tom arrive at their BBS station in an attempt to deliver their story. Never had a building looked so good. The big shining letters BBS glinted in the sun. They had made it out of the house with their story relatively intact. They had to hide for a few days to let things cool down. As they stood, waiting impatiently for the elevator, the lobby seemed a little more congested than the usual weekday traffic. People seemed to be whispering and were scurrying about in an unusual manner. The elevator doors finally opened. Out spilled the people, among them was Fran Staples, with a large manila envelope clutched tightly in her hands. Fran nearly knocked Shelly to the ground. Her attention wasn't facing forward. Instead, she was looking over her shoulder, worried and distracted.

"Geez, watch where you're going!" Shelly was knocked back against the wall.

"I'm sorry!" Fran's eyes were darting everywhere. She merely responded out of habit, not seeing the person she was talking to.

"Hey, are you all right?" It was obvious this woman was distracted.

"Yes, I'm terribly sorry." As Fran focused on the woman she had nearly run over, a light of recognition darted across her face. "Aren't you Shelly Cleveland, a reporter for the BBS?"

"Yes. Can I help you?"

"We can't talk here. There are FBI agents in the building. We have to go somewhere else." The conspiratorial sound of her voice was lost on Shelly. The only words she seemed to have heard were FBI agents.

Grabbing both women by the elbows, Tom ushered them out the front doors.

"I thought we would have a little more time than this!" Tom knew the agency was fast but for them to have made them so easily was unbelievable until he looked ahead of him at the van. "Talk about driving an advertisement!" He was disgusted at himself for being such a moron.

"I had no idea that things had gotten this bad at Aztec! How could they have known about the earnings statements? They have been kept from the employees, that's understandable, but how did the FBI know that the company was going to lie to all of us?" Fran was babbling out of nerves. Had the envelope in her hands been a hanky it would have been rung into a string by now. As it was, it was crumbled and nearly in shreds.

Shelly was confused. Between Tom's dragging them along like rag dolls, this woman's ranting, and the FBI, things seemed to be unraveling.

"Hold on!" Giving her arm a mighty jerk from Tom's grasp, she turned on Fran. "What are you talking about? Why would the FBI be looking for you? What does Aztec Motors have to do with them? What do you know about Jack Mason meeting with Vice President Holland?"

"I don't know anything about the Vice President meeting with Mason. All I know about is the company meeting we had where Mr. Mason lied to everyone about the company! They're going to start layoffs due to poor profits, but that's not true! We had one of the best quarters on record this year!" Fran suddenly clammed up. Maybe these weren't the people to be talking to. Perhaps she had made a terrible mistake, and the FBI would have been the ones to talk to. What had she done?

Seeing her fright, Tom stepped in with his calm, deep voice. "Why don't we all just take a breath? There's a coffee shop across the street. Let's go get some coffee and do some talking?"

CHAPTER 16

Senator Morrison sat in anticipation for the response from his republican colleagues. He and Peeling needed their endorsement before entering the race for President of the United States.

Morrison was getting frustrated as he attempted to put thoughts onto paper. They would be the ideas that would help America grow economically.

"This sounds terrible!" he mumbled to himself. Removing the sheet of paper that he was writing on, he frustratingly crunched the paper into a ball. Tossing it, it landed along side of the other twenty-two attempts.

Glancing in the mirror he studied his face. It looked worn. Streaks of gray were encroaching on his once jet-black hairline.

"*I can't believe that I'm doing this!*" he thought. "*Me President!*" Laughing a little, he finished his coffee.

"Excuse me, sir."

Morrison glanced over toward his door. There stood his aide, arms stacked with paperwork.

"Yes, what is it?"

"There's a Pastor here to see you. He claims it's important."

"They all say that." he said with a hint of cynicism. "Can't you just tell him that I'm busy?"

His sheepish smile disappeared as Pastor Hayes gently walked by his aid accidently, bumping his shoulder.

"I'm sorry Senator Morrison. I know that you're a busy man but this truly *is* important."

Senator Morrison looked over his room. For some reason it resembled Peeling's office he thought. He was embarrassed because of the clutter that filled all the open areas. Soda cans, old pizza boxes and, of course, paper balls previously crunched up from many bad ideas. As fast as he could, he made a humorous attempt at cleaning the room. Unfortunately, this also meant knocking over his coffee mug in the process.

"Let me help you." Hayes insisted as he began bending down picking up the paper balls that were laying about the floor. "Please don't worry about the mess, I do the very same thing." laughed Hayes.

At the end the two men stood facing each other each with their arms full. Morrison stood out between the two. It seemed almost comical watching him stand there with his arms filled with paper balls and his pants speckled with drops of coffee from the bottom of his coffee mug. You might say he resembled something between Red Skelton and Boris Karloff. Both men had a good laugh, something that was really needed about that time. The two men adjourned to the Senator's couch.

"Alright Pastor, how can I help you?"

"Senator, a very serious problem has risen, but I'm afraid when I tell you what it is, your going to find it hard to believe. First, let me tell you that I have discussed this with all the church leaders from the United Pentecostal Church. They all believe that you're the man I need to bring this to. Second, I've been in touch with the pastors from all the surrounding denominational churches in the D.C. area to discuss how we, as a body, can reach out to our neighbors. So many folks are losing their jobs and their homes. We have seen the homeless out there Senator! The streets are filled with people who are seeking refuge, and they are turning toward liquor stores for an answer instead of us. Senator, the people are slowly losing hope."

"I'm sorry, Pastor. I know that it's our fault."

Pastor Hayes abruptly interrupted. "Wait, Senator, let me finish. We, in the church, feel like we're to blame for not doing enough to reach out like we should. If we were doing more to bring Christ to the people, then, perhaps, that creature sitting in the Whitehouse wouldn't have been able to achieve what he has." "Pastor, what are you talking about? I don't agree with him on certain topics but calling our President a creature? Isn't that a little strong for a Pastor?"

"No, sir, not in this case. This is the part that you will find hard to believe. Senator, we have proof that they are doing diabolical things within the government and private sectors. They have a plan, Senator, to destroy our nation, as we know it! God told me Senator that you know it as well. I believe that you are one of the keys that will rid us of this demon once and for all!"

"Demon? You can't be serious!"

"Tell me, Senator, do you believe in God?"

"Yes sir, I do. I was raised in the Baptist church".

"Then you know that Jesus, himself, cast out demons. In Mark 5: 2-9 when they saw Jesus, they became so afraid that they cried and looked to be cast into a herd of pigs. We could spend the whole evening discussing this but whether you believe in demons or not, we can agree on one thing; that is, McChellan must not be allowed to have a second term in office. We are here because we believe that God wants you to run for the office. I believe, that if you run, you will win."

Senator Morrison was taken aback. How could he have known their plans for running?

"Pastor Hayes, did anyone tell you of our plans?"

Now Pastor Hayes held the puzzled expression.

"No Senator. As a church body we prayed morning, noon and night for the last three years waiting for an answer. We believe that this is God's plan for victory. Senator, I now see that it's more of a confirmation then a request. You were already planning to run, weren't you?" Reluctantly, the Senator began telling the Pastor what he and Senator Peeling discussed at his home the previous evening.

"I must warn you that once you begin this journey, you and your running mate are going to be in danger!

That man will do anything to win this time. He knows that we know about him and his plans."

"I want to show you something Pastor." Senator Morrison walked to his bookcase and returned with an oddly covered book. The book's cover was very old and had many different bright colors that dimmed with age. The printing was set in bronze.

"It's my favorite book!" replied Morrison with a big smile. Pastor Hayes took the book from the Senator. He began to read., To his amazement he found the text was written in Hebrew. Suddenly, his eyes grew wide and a smile of recognition blossomed on his lips. He looked up at the Senator. This was a bible! "I've never seen one like this before!"

The expression on the Pastor's face drew a laugh from Morrison. "Some politicians do read it from time to time! I must admit, not as much as we should." Morrison knew that everything the Pastor was saying made some sense but, demons? He still wasn't convinced about that. Yet, how did he know about their plans to run? That concerned him. So he decided to play along and find out more of what the Pastor knew. If anything, he surely would want the support of the Christian community.

"Everything you said is inline with everything that has happened these past few months. I've received documents from people I've never heard of before. Strange things have been taking place within the Congress and the Senate. Bills are being past without going through normal protocol, even the secret service and the military police have been following government officials to their homes. They just sit there watching our every move. Pastor, I physically have seen everything that you say is happening. I'm a rational man, I believe I know what is real and what is not real. What is good, and what is bad. I must say, in all honesty, the man is a bad president, but hardly a demon."

"I will tell you this, there have been many of our members coming to me claiming they see strange dark shadow type things floating around the Whitehouse and the President himself. Some say it's more like smoke. Dark smoke that follows him and remains with him but, only certain people can see it."

Suddenly the Senator's mind raced back to the night when Senator Peeling escaped through his egress window from his basement. He remembered the dark smoke that surrounded his home. He also remembered that the smoke had no actual smell to it. Just coincidence?"

Morrison began to feel the hairs on the back of his neck begin to stand, *how could this be*? "The other evening I may have seen that smoky thing. Senator Peeling was at my home for a private meeting. Peeling had to run threw it to leave. Come to think of it, it didn't set off any of the smoke alarms!" Morrison looked at Pastor Hayes with concern. He was begin-ning to wonder. "Tell me more about this smoke. I know a BBS reporter who told me of her first encounter with it and McChellan."

"By chance would that reporter's last name be Cleveland?"

"You know her?"

"Her name has been mentioned many times in some of the documents I received. She seems to get around."

Pastor Hayes, seemingly surprised by how informed Morrison already was, continued talking. "McChellan was stepping out of his limousine and the inside of the car seemed to be filled with the smoke. No one seemed alarmed by this. Why? All the people who came forth and claimed they saw the smoke are good, honest people. God has confirmed to me that everything I said here tonight is true. He has provided us a plan for deliverance. You will be playing a vital roll in this nation's recovery. There's a small a scripture that comes to mind."

Using the Senator's oddly colored bible, he gently flipped through the pages. Finding the Book of Psalms, Chapter 7, verse 9, Pastor Hayes began to read aloud. "Oh let the wickedness of the wicked come to an end; but establish the just: for the righteous God trieth the hearts and reigns."

"Nathanial." Morrison's voice was now somber. A new respect for this man of God arose within him that brought the two men to a first name basis. "Deep down I knew that there was something evil about McChellan by the way he influences people. I've known it for years. It was just too unlikely for good, honest people, ones that I've known for years, who stood by their beliefs for so long, to suddenly change after one conversation with our President. Something is very wrong. I still don't know if it's demons or drugs. We need to find out what it is, and put an end to it now, while we still have an opportunity. Pastor, there is something you should know before it gets to be public knowledge. There are bills right now scheduled to go before the senate concerning where and when people will be allowed to practice their faith. Should they pass, your young friends outside the Whitehouse, may be in trouble."

Just then the office door opened and Senator Peeling rushed in. "Senator Morrison, they turned you down, they won't endorse you."

"Who then? I haven't heard any other names mentioned, and someone needs to start campaigning now!"

"Find a way William! Hayes interjected. God is on your side, you cannot lose." Morrison looked at Hayes sternly, then after a moment, he turned to Senator Peeling. "You are my running mate Thomas!" Peeling stood there with a stunned expression on his face, "Me?"

"Yes! You. We run as independents understand! Get the papers filed. Plan on spending the evening. We have work to do."

As the two Senators began discussing their campaign strategies, Pastor Hayes knew he was out of the conversation. Quietly he walked over to Morrison's desk to leave him a little message. Removing a sheet of paper from his notebook he wrote, Colossians 1:9-10 for this cause we also, since the day we heard it, do not cease to pray for you! And to desire that ye might be filled with the knowledge of his will in all wisdom and spiritual understanding, that ye might walk worthy of the Lord into all pleasing, being fruitful in every good work, and increasing in the knowledge of God.

Pastor Hayes walked over and placed his hand on Morrison's shoulder. The two men stopped talking and gave their attention to the Pastor.

"Before I leave I wanted to invite you both to our church meeting next Saturday. It will be held at St Mary's. People from every denomination will be there. Bring your proof, tell them what you know, and remember who is on your side. I will always be there should you need me."

Pastor Hayes turned and left the office. Peeling, feeling a little confused by the stranger, asked Morrison, "Who was that? Morrison softly placed his hand on bible then responded, "God's hand."

CHAPTER 17

It was evening in D.C. Frost was covering the tree branches creating a beautiful shine when the moonlight kissed their branches. Fred and Esther couldn't help but notice the beauty, and just marveled at the sight.

"Isn't God's creation beautiful?" asked Esther. Her face held a glow of it's own, matching the beauty of the trees. It glowed with a joy that only God provided when His Spirit moved within her.

"Are you sure God did this? Doesn't Mother Nature get a little credit?" replied Fred with a playful smile.

Esther, always ready to defend God, reached into her purse feeling around for her bible in case he really wanted to debate this area of thought. She stopped, and realized whom she was with and decided that perhaps a little patience was needed more than the on coming argument. In the past, Fred would have simply agreed with her. Every now and then, in Fred's presence, she felt a kind of conflict in her spirit. It was as if she felt terribly uncomfortable and wanted him nowhere near her. Esther was surprised that Fred had returned, especially wanting to go out. Esther wanted to know more of where he was, and what he was, perhaps, there was, no time like the present.

Earlier, they both enjoyed dining and discussing old times. Taking a walk in the park was unexpected for her, she was not prepared for it. First, she wasn't dressed for the cold, and second, just what did he have in mind?

Esther never thought about Fred romantically before because her mind was so focused on Marcus. One thing was for sure, if he did have ideas about dating, views like the one he just spoke of were out of line as far as she was concerned. She was taken back by his comment about God, even though he claimed he was joking, some jokes were not funny to her his version on creation really made her wonder, just where did he stand when it came to God? At one time she thought she knew.

"Fred I loved that restaurant, the old world atmosphere was wonderful, and the pizza was amazing."

Finally a smile crossed Fred's face. "It reminded me of when my aunt took me to pizza places in Chicago. It was the best pizza!" he replied while licking his lips wildly and rubbing his stomach. His act was convincing, to a point.

The creature inside him hated every second of it, acting like this weak small person made him feel pathetic. He knew his master and what would lie ahead if he were to stop now! He needed something, just that certain something that would just grab Esther's attention and keep it, allowing him to be able to obtain the information McChellan demanded. Finally, their stories reached a point where they both had tears of laughter. "Fred it's O.K, I'm glad to see that you are becoming your old self again."

Fred directed the conversation toward the lookout tower the rangers used to watch over the park. Esther looked up at him a little frightened. "Do you think it's alright? She asked timidly.

Fred began to laugh almost to the point of rudeness. "Why are you laughing at me?" Esther responded with a hint of coldness.

Noticing the alarm in her voice, Fred gently took her hand, and quickly changed the mood.

Again the creature began stirring. Gentleness and kindness was not in its character. Allowing these emotions to surface was causing it great discomfort and made Fred seem more and more awkward and insincere.

"Come on lets go" he said softly, "by reaching the top of the tower we will be able to see the whole park", making sure to emphasize on the beauty of the moon light on the trees.

They walked to the hand railing and began the climb to the top.

"Wow replied Esther, the city seems alive tonight!"

"It is beautiful." he whispered as he snuggled in a little closer. Sliding his arm around hers and interlocked them.

Esther began feeling very uneasy about the whole situation. She loved the idea of being friends with Fred.

But he was acting so odd that it seemed as if he was a total stranger. How could anyone change that much?

"Fred I think you can take me home now!" she responded abruptly.

Fred knew that he blew it. He knew that McChellan was counting on him and he couldn't let the night end until he got the information he wanted.

In one motion, Fred came after her, "Come on!" He shouted, what was supposed to have been a soft and warm response came out as a loud shout that alarmed even him. The creature inside of him was ready to lunge at Esther, but Fred turned the whole scenario into a soft apology. Once again Fred reached out for her, and again the creature reacted. He came at her with a fierceness that intimidated her, causing her to jump away from him.

Esther was causing all kinds of problems for Fred that evening. He knew that if he didn't get back to McChellan with the information he wanted, undoubtedly his life would be shortened by a number of years. With Fred the creature had found a way to hide itself from the eyes of this young Christian woman. There was one thing evil hadn't counted on, and that was the creature itself couldn't stay very close to Esther or, for that matter, anyone who had the Holy Spirit for a prolonged length of time. The creature would soon begin to act out uncontrollably disclosing itself, making it impossible for the creature to use this trick a second time.

"Ok. I'll take you home!" He quickly caught up to her and tried to grasp her hand, but she pulled it away.

"No Fred! Don't! I'm not interested in you that way." Fred stepped back. He knew he needed a new tactic. Fred became humble. He needed to come up with a lie and he knew it had to be a good one.

"Esther, I'm sorry if I seem strange to you. The real reason I was gone for so long," he paused for a moment then blurted out, "was I was being treated for depression."

"I've been so alone and I just thought that since you weren't with Marcus anymore, then perhaps, maybe?"

Esther had become strong in her walk with the Lord. She was nobody's doormat. She understood Christ's teachings well, and that's what he was counting on, forgiveness. After a few minutes, and some well-placed lies, it worked. She softened and took his hand.

"If you knew God like I do, you wouldn't make jokes about his word", she whispered back softly. Smiling, Fred opened the car door and helped her in.

Reaching Esther's home, Fred looked at Esther with genuine sincerity. "This God you seem to know so well, how about introducing him to me?" Esther sat back and studied his face to see if he was poking fun again.

"O.K., Fred, tell you what, there's a church meeting this weekend, come with me!"

Fred, realizing he struck gold, played it cool. "What time?" he asked softly.

"8:00 Saturday evening. You don't have to dress up, just come with an open mind!"

"It's a date." he said softly.

After walking Esther to her door, he returned to his car and began his drive home. After two blocks Fred pulled his car over to the curb. Making sure no one was watching, he pulled his cell phone from his pocket and dialed.

"I'm in! I'll report everything after the meeting." After Fred hung up the phone the creature inside of him responded with delight placing a huge smile of success upon his face.

CHAPTER 18

Saturday evening finally arrived. This evening was meant to be the evening of evenings for two special parties each with a great deal on the line.

Perhaps needs would finally be met and answers provided. This was the night everyone had been waiting for and, yes, that even included President McChellan.

People of many different faiths began arriving from all over the state to hear what six simple pastors had in mind to help their communities. Many were there to hear from the two senators that were creating such a fuss throughout capital hill and the rest of the country.

The auditorium was huge. The building, itself, was truly beautiful. Throughout the structure five large rooms were built, each with large domed ceilings. Crystal chandlers were placed in odd shapes so masterfully that not only did they create a most beautiful angelic glow over the congregation but also, the lighting provided a warm visual effect on the many different pieces that had been hand painted by the masters over the years. Secondary lighting was used around the stain glass windows to elegantly display the history of their church's biblical teachings.

The floors were all made of hard wood, polished to a bright shine so no matter where you walked nothing but the finest quality was portrayed.

Fred gazed over all the people entering the building almost as if he were looking for someone in particular.

"Wow! I didn't know these guys had such a following!"

"Yes! Isn't this great!" Esther replied. This night her spirits were high. The evening coolness caused her cheeks to redden just slightly making her smile glow. Her reaction caught everyone's attention.

"I think it's wonderful that all the churches are finally getting together and doing something for the people."

Fred grimaced from Esther's reaction. To him little goodie two shoes was being just a little too joyful for him. The creature inside of him found it revolting almost to the point of being unbearable. "No! He replied, "It's not the churches I'm concerned with."

Upon entering the building they were greeted by friendly out going ushers handing out bulletins that described the evening's events.

The crowd was huge; people were bumping and pushing their way down the hallway toward the seating area. Esther and Fred struggled their way through the crowd.

"Fred can you see my Mother? She is saving seats for us." Gazing over the huge crowd, Fred located Esther's mother, Mary. She was sitting alone up front close to the stage.

It was going to be difficult reaching her, so many people were standing in the isle chatting but they wanted to be seated before the meeting began. This was going to require a bit of imagination to get there.

Esther wanted time to discuss a matter with Mary before the activities began but, by the size of the crowd, that looked highly improbable. The two looked the situation over and, as if by magic, they both seemed to share the same idea. Esther reached out to him. "Do we dare?" she asked trembling.

"The crowd noise was so deafening he had to yell. She could barely hear him. Both of them knew it was now or never. The two took the chance and began climbing. They climbed over the seats row by row much to the annoyance of the crowd. Until, at last, they reached row seven.

Instantly, Mary leapt to her feet and welcomed them.

"I'm so glad you two could be here, The meeting is very important to our whole community. We all need to get involved."

A loud pounding began to echo throughout the halls of the large auditorium commanding the people's attention.

"Please, before we begin I think it's right for us to ask God for his direction in this meeting."

Everyone stood as Pastor Hayes let loose with one of his powerful prayers that left everyone with that tingly feeling on the back of their necks. "I'd like to take this time to thank Father O'Hara for allowing us to use this beautiful auditorium. Without it, a meeting of this size could not have taken place."

A loud applause rang out across the room. Soon the crowd quieted. Pastor Hayes continued, "I'd like to introduce our Pastors."

One by one, each pastor was introduced, each strong in their convictions, each proud to be a member of a team that is helping so many people in a time of need. Pastor Seaford from Trinity Lutheran Church, Pastor Adams from United Methodist and Pastor Jaspers from the Community Church. Father O'Hara from St Mary's Catholic Church, and I'm Pastor Hayes from Christ's Sword United Pentecostal Church."

After the applause quieted down, Pastor Hayes opened his Bible, "In the book of Matthew Chapter 25 beginning with verse 35, Jesus said that when he was thirsty you gave him drink, when he was hungry, you gave him food, when he didn't have clothing, you clothed him. Jesus was referring to our brothers and sisters out there who are hungry and homeless and desperate for help! Many have lost their jobs and are losing their homes. As I walked down the streets in my neighborhood, I see many people who are sitting outside storefronts seemingly without hope, wondering where their next meal is going to come from. These are good, decent people not looking for handouts, just a little help. Jesus finished by saying, when helping the hungry and the homeless, you have indeed done it unto him! I believe that unless we do something to help our fellow man, the Lord, himself, will hold us accountable."

A loud applause rang out within the auditorium, the other five Pastors all stood, worshiped God, and gave thanks. As the applause quieted, Pastor Hayes continued, "Each church was given a huge undertaking. When completed, it should help hundreds of people in need over the next 6 years. I'd like to ask each Pastor to come up now and provide a detailed plan of what their respective church will undertake and what each plan will cover, such as costs and actual manpower. I'd first like to ask Pastor Jeffery Seaford, the Senior Pastor of Trinity Lutheran Church, to come up first and address this congregation."

Walking up to the podium a young man in his thirties took the microphone from Pastor Hayes.

"Thank you Pastor Hayes and welcome all of you to this very important meeting. This council has decided to appoint to each church body within the Lutheran Church of Washington, a special and unique task, one that each church will be accountable for. We have the honor of starting new food pantries throughout the D.C. area. This means we will expect commitments from all persons within our respective congregations to help out. We need to make this work!"

Pastor Seaford went on explaining the locations of the new pantries and the money that will be required for the operation. He explained that the Lutheran Church was selected for the larger of the projects because of the size of their congregations. It was decided that it would be less of a burden on the larger of the churches then on the churches in the area with smaller congregations.

Knowing this would draw many questions, Pastor Seaford swayed the emotion of the moment toward the next Pastor, and quickly introduced Charles Adams, Pastor of United Methodist Church.

Pastor Adams shared his plans for new homeless shelters around the area, and then in turn was followed by the final group of Pastors, all following suit. Finally, after two hours, Pastor Hayes was brought back to the podium for the question and answer period.

These Pastors knew this was going to be tough and very difficult to convince the members of their respective congregations to go along with these ideas. They also knew the importance of these programs and the effects they hope to achieve from them. So, for now, they were willing to put up with the struggle.

The questions came hard and right to the point. They were answered, honestly and directly. When it was finally time to call for a break, both sides seemed ready for one. Approaching the podium, Pastor Hayes stood wiping perspiration from his forehead. "We have now completed the first half of this program. We are hopeful that you, as members of God's body, understand the urgency of getting these programs started. Please begin to pray for a burden and get involved. Helping is sharing. The second part of this meeting will begin in fifteen minutes. The two young senators have exciting news to share with you. Please come on back. You're excused in Jesus' name."

CHAPTER 19

The lights went on, the murmur of the crowd became a roar as the people began leaving their seats rushing toward the refreshment stands and the restrooms. The hallway was filled with people and cigarette smoke was all around. Esther coughed over and over again rubbing her eyes from the burning as she walked toward the restroom door. The smell of hairspray escaped from the crease along the bottom of the doorway, many vulgarities came from the mouths of some who felt it the appropriate time to voice their concerns and displeasures with their pastor's decisions. Esther decided now was not the best time for entering, instead, she decided on doing a little exploring. At the end of the hall a huge crowd gathered at one of the far exit doors.

She witnessed two large men pushing and shoving each other, arguing over some political topic. Esther moved closer, trying to figure out what was happening, but, as she reached the area, two ushers stepped in to halt the argument. A third usher came from behind, took hold of Esther's arm, and escorted her back to the Isle that led to her seat.

"What were they arguing about?" Esther asked inquisitively. "I really don't know! Something about the health care bill. I guess the other guy didn't agree with his view." He could tell by the expression on her face that she was unfamiliar with the latest gossip from Washington.

"You don't know about the health care bill? It's been in all the papers, really doesn't matter, the bill never passed. But I guess it meant a lot to that guy in the blue shirt".

Halfway down the isle Esther noticed that Fred was missing. Mary was standing pointing toward the exit door. Esther knew something was wrong. Fred was wrong; everything about Fred was messed up. Esther knew he was in trouble somehow. Why would he just get up and leave, especially out a side emergency door? If he wanted to leave, why didn't he just use the main exit? Her curiosity was now set aflame and she hurried toward the side exit. Approaching the door she began waving her hands frantcally in the air, acting faint and in need of air. Reaching the door she explained to the usher that she felt over heated and needed some fresh air. He opened the door but reminded her that the meeting would begin soon. Esther hesitantly walked out, slowly at first pondering her surroundings. Then she began walking up and down the alley. She didn't see Fred anywhere. From a distance, she heard voices coming from around the corner. Cautiously, Esther moved toward the edge of the nearby building. Peeking her head around the corner, she noticed Fred. He was talking to three strange looking people, two men and one women. The people were dressed, in her opinion oddly. The woman's shirt did resemble hers, but had what seemed to be bright red blotches that covered much of the front half of the shirt. All three wore jeans, but the men alone wore orange strips on their white tea shirts. The woman's shirt however, stood out more than anything else to Esther. What was all that red?

Then Esther noticed Fred handing them something, it was black and it seemed to move up their arms like smoke, encircling their bodies. Esther was shocked by what she had just witnessed. She remembered the evening in the park and now, there it was again, only this time with Fred. Frightened, she turned quickly not taking into account what was around her. She smacked a garbage can that was sitting along side her. Esther reached out quickly and grabbed the handle before it could fall. However, the lid slid down along the side of the building making a muffled scrapping sound.

Esther looked up quickly, "Oh! They had to have heard that" she murmured. Hearing the sound of footsteps quickly approaching, she let go of everything and ran as fast as she could to get back to the door. She began pounding, again and again, with the palm of her hand. She knew she couldn't pound too loud, without drawing Fred's attention, then again, who cared! He was coming anyway! She needed to get in *NOW*!

Glancing over to the corner of the building she could hear footsteps approaching, her heart was beating as if it would burst through her chest. Then suddenly the door opened and Esther rushed through the door knocking the usher to the floor. Esther kept running until she found her mother Mary. Totally out of breath, she flopped down in her seat still trying to come to terms with what she had just witnessed. "Mom you won't believe what I just saw!" Just as Esther was about to begin telling Mary what she just witnessed, Mary looked up in time to see Fred walking down the isle and quickly placed her forefinger to Esther's lips, quietly silencing her daughter with a sign language explanation.

"Miss me!" he asked loudly, almost sounding angry.

Esther jumped in her seat, "Fred! You're back!"

"I'm glad I made it back in time. I didn't want to miss Morrison."

Esther noticed a change. There was something different about Fred. He was smiling.

CHAPTER 20

The lights began to dim and the crowd silenced. Pastor Adams walked up to the podium. "Ladies and gentlemen we the churches of this great community have developed a plan to aid our neighbors, but what about our hurting nation? Tonight, it is my honor to introduce two men who have taken precious time out of their busy schedules to come and address our respective congregations. Tonight, not only are they here to share in our plans, they have also come to address the problems this nation is suffering as a whole. They are here to open our eyes and to provide some rather startling information. All we ask is that you listen with an open mind. Please welcome from the State of Texas, Independent candidate for President of the United States, Senator William Morrison, and from the State of Wisconsin, the Vice Presidential candidate, Senator Thomas Peeling."

A huge applause exploded across the auditorium. Morrison reached down and took Peeling's wrist and the two together, raised their arms for victory. As the applause lessened, the two senators began by putting up enlarged charts. Each chart had enlarged prints of documents and photographs. Senator Peeling left the room for a few minutes while Senator Morrison took his cue and addressed the crowd.

He began with his plan for the economy and why his plan would increase employment by as much as 30% in the first year alone. Morrison explained that part of his plan was to lower industrial taxes, making it easier for businesses to remain, and keep jobs in the area. At the same time this would open doors for new business to enter, and be successful.

Senator Peeing arrived back on stage pushing a large flat screen television with DVD player on the cart.

Morrison spoke boldly throughout his presentation with encouragement for the future, reaching out to all the people who were living on near to nothing.

Finally, they came to the part of their presentation they dreaded most of all. They knew the information they were about to disclose had to be given with kid gloves. It was the reason they chose to run even if it meant leaving their party. It was why they feared so for the nation and, yes, it was make or break time. It was either convince the people that they really knew what they were talking about or give the country back into the hands of the two men sitting in the office and hope for the best.

In the months before this meeting, both of the Senators lives, and those of their families, had been threaten many times. Morrison and Peeling never once backed down knowing what was at stake. Times were made difficult during the campaign when money ran short. It seemed as if they were getting no support from anyone or, for that matter, anywhere. It seemed that the only people who had shown even a remote interest in what they were saying, came from small rebellious groups that thrived over the internet or other types of small insignificant computer geek groups, only providing low numbers at best. Many nights the Senators wondered if they, in fact, committed political suicide. Where were all these so called Christian groups that were going to come to their support?

Now thing's would be different, they were in D.C. This city was special when it came to election miracles. Morrison knew the people here always seemed to have their finger on the pulse of the society. If anyone would know that they were being taken for fools, it had to be them.

Peeling felt reluctant about bringing out the charts that he was about to present. He knew that these people worked hard for a living and had families. They never deserved what had happed to them. Peeling knew that by telling them, it was going to anger them. He also knew that tonight, government, true honest government, will lose what little trust the people had in it. This trust had to be restored.

He really didn't want to hurt these people but the truth had to come out. The documents on the charts proved how the auto manufactures purposely misled the public with gross under estimated figures and reporting of the profits. What worried Peeling the most was that everywhere he and Morrison went no one seemed to believe them. Now it was up to him to sell it the best way he knew how, the only way he knew how, straight, honest. However, would they listen? No matter the out come, they deserved to know the truth. Peeling went straight into explaining the government's Wall Street cover up. He explained how Wall Street firms in conjunction with the CEO's of major manufacturing companies, swindled many of them out of their retirement plans. Peeling spoke for two hours, delivering detail upon detail. Peeling shared with them pictures and graphs that outlined numbers. Peeling feared, many people didn't understand all the information he had crammed into two hours. Many were bored with the presentation after the first hour, waiting anxiously for the refreshment all in all, it left the people confused and asking questions among themselves.

The crowd grew very silent, and then murmurings arose from the back. Shouts of anger came from many sections, causing the ushering staff to be on their guard. Senator Morrison held up his hands, "Please! Let us finish!" Then we will be glad to answer any questions that you may have!" Senator Peeling waved to the back and the ushers began handing out prepared packets. Each folder contained copies of the original documents that were being explained up on the stage.

"The Packets that we prepared for you will provide you with proof that the auto industries actually made money the year before they claimed bankruptcy! We can tell you that an Aztec employee, who worked for them for many years provided these documents. The other papers were all sent to us from other sources, including the Whitehouse."

All six pastors got up and walked over to the chart with the enlarged prints. "This is awful" cried Father O'Hara, "You're telling us that this administration purposely misled the people!"

"Up to a certain point, Father. At first we believed that it was just something the auto industrialists were involved with, but then all the paper companies in the north began to fail in the same way, each making huge profits. By the year's end, they made huge layoffs followed by either filing bankruptcy or they picked up and moved to a different country claiming that the tax burdens were too high. We didn't know that this administration was involved until we received these!" Holding up his hand, the Senator held three different documents. "Please turn to page sixteen in your booklet, you will see pictures of Vice President Holland secretly speaking to the heads of Ashford Investments the Wall Street giant and the leaders of two major auto industrialists in the United States! Upon hearing a recorded conversation between these men, we knew that a plan was made with the full knowledge of this administration."

"You are good, hard working people, who should never have lost your jobs!"

Father O'Hara looked at Morrison puzzled. "Why? Why would they do such a thing?"

"They needed to get a bill passed last month. You may know it as the stimulus bill. Which, by the way, was passed just last month!" replied Peeling

Pastor Jaspers interrupted the Senator "Yes! But, won't that help the business' get back on their feet?"

Senator Morrison placed his laser pointer down on the table and turned toward the people. "Ladies and gentlemen, with this bill the government can issue loans to all companies, big or small, that need a little boost to keep their businesses afloat. But, please remember, that the stimulus money is a loan and by agreeing to the terms of the government contract, this government will now have a say as to what happens within your business, and how it's to be run!"

"Let's try some simple math. We know that Wall Street collapsed. They took a loan. Then, the auto industrialists filed for bankruptcy and they took a loan. Fedway, the mortgage giant, needed money for home loans. They took a loan. The huge steel and paper plants all filed for bankruptcy, and they also took out loans! Now this administration is working toward controlling our health care!"

"Add that up! They now control all finance, all industry, all real state, and even many small business'!" Glancing back at Father O'Hara he softly replied, "That is why father, they want control!"

Pastor Jaspers grew angry and made his feelings known, "Your talking conspiracy!" he shouted, "I won't have anything to do with this!" With that he stormed back to his seat. The crowd erupted! Shouting began through out the building. Pastors Hayes and Adams hurried to the front in an attempt to quiet the crowd. The ushers began moving down the isles trying to regain control. After a few minutes, cool heads prevailed. Finally the crowd simmered down and everyone returned to their seats. Father O'Hara sat with Pastor Jaspers trying his best to calm him.

Senator Peeling took a deep steadying breath to calm down before he spoke. They were blessed. This was the final meeting of a life-time and all the right words were coming out. It's his turn to address the assembly and failure was not an option.

"Senator Morrison and I both agree that if these companies would just bring back their employees, they could restart at anytime! Small business failed because the larger businesses believed that Wall Street collapsed. The documents we have provided prove that Wall Street never really collapsed. Therefore, all that money they claimed is missing, is still there, waiting to be used! Senator Morrison and I will do everything in our power to find that money and get it flowing again. This will strengthen our economy once again."

Morrison stepped up boldly taking the lead. "We believe that it's the people, Hard working people, that are the backbone of this nation. We believe that government should work for the people, not the other way around. It's you, the workers, who are the real strength of this nation! It's through your faith in God, hard work, and a strong commitment to succeed and to each other, that is what formed this nation!"

A loud applause broke out across the auditorium. Esther James glanced over at Fred and noticed that he wasn't smiling anymore.

"I know many of you wanted to see the President's health care bill get passed!" replied Morrison, "Let me explain why my running mate Senator Peeling performed the filibuster the other day to postpone it."

"First, to pay for it they wanted to cut Medicare by ten percent. That means the elderly would lose many of their benefits, also, a persons right to the doctor of their choice was in question. What if you needed a special procedure done and the agency contracted by the government decided that it was too expensive? What then? The second reason was this," turning on the DVD player blueprints appeared on the screen. "Recently we received proof that this administration has begun construction on a new chain of clinics across the country! We now know that these clinics are being built for the direct purpose of studying human cloning and stem cell research! You may remember that the President has stated that he was against this monstrous procedure. As you can see, that's not true. What's more, we know he intended to use money from your health care coverage to finance these buildings! If you wish to know more about this research, it's in the booklet we handed out. Or, come up and view all our other documents and view the DVD."

The crowd began paging through the book and gasped! Loud murmuring spread like wildfire across the room. This time the people sat back stunned at what these two senators were saying!

"I've had enough!" Pastor Jaspers declared, and he and Pastor Seaford stormed toward the two Senators. Pastors Hayes and Adams were right behind them holding onto them the best they could.

"How do we know you didn't create this stuff?" Shouted, Jaspers, "I'm with him on this one!" added Seaford. "To believe that the President of the United States would actually hurt the people of this country like this! I can't believe it! How do we know that their proof is real?"

From the corner of the stage came a woman carrying a medium sized cardboard box. Moving like a person on a mission, she moved quietly through the shadows until she approached the stage stairs. As she climbed the steps, the room became very quiet. The people were eager to hear what this woman had to say. Who was this woman?

"My name is Jill Rafferity and I know President McChellan personally!"

Jaspers backed away, actually fearing for his life. The Senator's security began closing in on the stranger but Morrison stopped them, recognizing her immediately.

A quite murmur began to spread across the assembly. "I was his campaign manager during the last election, and I can tell you, this is real!" She handed the box to Pastor Hayes then stood to the side and waited for what was to come. She stood bold and confident. She knew this was the end of her career and possibly her life.

"Please, Pastor, open the box and show this man what's inside!"

Pastor Hayes removed the lid very carefully and removed seven documents each with the Presidential Seal stamped on the cover.

Pastor Hayes looked sternly at Jaspers. "They couldn't possibly have faked this," pointing to the Seal.

Jaspers took the documents and began to read the first few paragraphs in each file trying desperately to find something to prove them wrong. These were from the President himself. How could the man he so respected have done something like this? Now he felt foolish which made everything seem worse. What was everyone going to think? He felt foolish and prideful. Pastor Jaspers gave back the documents and he returned to his seat, shattered.

Pastor Adams followed in an effort to comfort him. Pastor Jaspers placed his hands over his face in embarrassment. "I can't believe I acted like that! I just can't believe it!"

Esther James tired of hearing all the arguing from both sides, decided to step out and stretch her legs. Standing in the hallway she noticed the two men and the women that Fred had been speaking with in the alley. For some reason they were dressed differently. The men were now all dressed in black from head to toe.

Curiosity got the better of her again as she watched the three separate and move to different sections of the auditorium.

She watched until they finally mixed in with the others. *"It was unusual. Why the clothes change. Why all the secrecy? I wish Dad were here, maybe I should tell Pastor?"* she thought as she returned to her seat. She wanted to tell her mother what she had just seen, but Fred was back and she knew the timing was bad.

"Welcome back, are you having a problem?" he asked, as if he knew she was spying on him. Esther simply smiled and sat down between her mother and this man who was being so mysterious. Things were happening that didn't seem to add up. *What was he up too?*

Back up on stage, Pastor Hayes escorted Jill Rafferity over to the section where they were seated and the Senators began finishing up their part in the meeting.

Senator Morrison was finishing his talk about a new abortion process that was taking place in hospitals across the nation on the taxpayers dime, when suddenly all the entry doors burst open. Police, dressed in riot gear, entered forcefully, pushing people to the floor. Alarmed the people began leaving their chairs.

Police with megaphones shouted, "Remain in your seats!" Without a word Fred jumped out of his and hurried down the isle.

Esther and Mary turned to see what the police would do to him. To their amazement the police just let Fred go right on through.

"Did you see that?"

"Please mom, this whole day has been weird."

The two women sat back silent and just watched as the police began moving up and down the isles. People were hurt laying face down on the floor.

Senator Morrison followed by Father O'Hara jumped off the stage and confronted the officer in charge.

"What's the meaning of this?" Father O'Hara demanded! "My name is Sergeant Gill of the D.C. Police Dept, just one hour ago two men and a woman entered a clinic over on Fifth Avenue shot and killed two of the doctors on duty."

"Witnesses said they saw the three suspects leave the group of protesters, from across the street, and enter the clinic.

"So what does that have to do with us?" Exclaimed father O'Hara."

"Two of the witnesses followed them here."

Father O'Hara was taken aback. "These people are from our respective congregations! We know each and everyone of them. I know none of them could do such a thing!" Sergeant Gill called for the witness to come in. "Alright point them out." Climbing on the stage, two men dressed in black looked over the crowd.

Esther was surprised at what she saw and turned to her mother. Those were the same two men that were with that woman in the hallway!

"There's one of them!" proclaimed one of the two men, pointing into the crowd.

The police pushed their way into the crowd and grabbed a man wearing jeans and a tea shirt with orange strips from the crowd, and placed him in handcuffs. Father O'Hara stopped them in the isle "What's your name son?" The frightened man looked at the father.

"Clarence Banks." replied the man. The Father lovingly placed his hand on his shoulder,

"Did you do this son?"

"No, father, I swear I never left here."

Pulling him away from Father O'Hara, the officer ordered him to be taken downtown. Then another man was pulled from the crowd, but he didn't go quietly. He swung wildly, punching anyone wearing blue. He kicked and bit his way through five police officers before they finally threw him to the floor and handcuffed him. By this time the officers were a little miffed. So instead of standing the man up to walk, they dragged him by his hair across the hardwood floor, straight out the closest exit. All the while, the man was screaming his innocence. Esther whispered to Mary, "*That's odd, he had on a white tea shirt with orange strips, just like the other man in the alley with Fred.*" Realizing the danger her daughter was in, Mary tightened her grip on Esther's hand.

The final witness, a woman dressed all in black, jumped up on the stage and began looking in all directions. Then suddenly, she began pointing wildly in Esther's direction, "There's the other one, by that lady!" Esther got pale. That person was pointing at her. She couldn't believe it! Why was she pointing at her, she didn't do anything! People all around them began screaming and closing in the isles trying to provide time for Mary and Esther to do something, anything!

Mary stood and held Esther tight. Mary whispered in her ear. "Listen to me! I know that you're scared, but you need to get out of here, "*now*!" Do you understand! Just wait until I tell you, and then run to that exit." Esther clung to her mother tightly. Right now their eye contact spoke more words between them then either of them could express openly. Mary had one more chance to speak to her daughter and clung to Esther with all her strength. "This is part of God's plan, he's your protection. He is always with you, trust in him!" Then reluctantly released her daughter.

"Where shall I go?"

"Fran's house! Go to Fran's house, she will help you." This was all Mary could say, the police were closing in. Pastor Hayes saw who was being accused and moved in to help.

Pastor Hayes loved each member of his congregation equally, but Esther had an integral part to play in the plan.

Hayes needed to act, and act he did. The Pastor leapt off the stage and let out a shout at the top of his lungs. "Stop! It couldn't be her," he yelled with all his might, "I've seen her here all night!" The officer looked sternly at the Pastor, "Are you sure? Pastor, your telling me that throughout this entire meeting she never once left your sight?"

Pastor Hayes knew that she did leave at the halfway mark of the meeting. She may have gone to the restroom, but not for an hour.

"That young man claimed that she left quite a few times, he claimed, that he was seated next to her. How do you explain that Pastor?"

Pastor Hayes saw Fred standing in the corner of the building watching. Pastor Hayes eyes were staring toward Fred. He now understood Fred, and what lived in Fred, so his choice was clear. He also realized this was part of God's plan and he was messing it up. He turned to Esther and shouted, "Run Now!" He himself ran and knocked one of the officers to the floor with his body. Mary and seven others encircled Esther and pushed their way down the isle until Esther reached the exit door and escaped.

Inside the police arrested Pastor Hayes and Mary James with aiding a wanted criminal. As they were leaving, Senator Morrison stepped in, using the power of his office to have them released in his custody, "Pastor Hayes, I suppose you know what you were doing! Right?"

"Senator those people are innocent, that young frightened girl would have never had a fair trial."

Jill Rafferity approached the two men.

"Senator Morrison didn't you recognize that young man?" She moved in a little closer and whispered "That's Fred Joiner!" Morrison looked at her puzzled, "Who?"

"That's President McChellan's personal secretary!"

Pastor Hayes was stunned at her reply. He was the fellow that had begun dating Esther. "I remember when they hung out as college students, did you know that she was once engaged to Marcus Holland until power overcame his senses."

"I guess that explains the frame up!"

"Pastor, I'm a lowly senator but I promise you this, I'm going to have that man investigated." "Ms Rafferity you came to my rescue once again, how can I help you?"

"I need a place to hide, until this thing is over with."

"I'll set you up. Just leave that up to me."

Leaving the two, Pastor Hayes rejoined Pastors Paulson and Adams on the floor trying to calm down many of the people. The crowd dispersed and went home leaving the four pastors sitting, pondering their next move.

"Gentlemen there is more going on here then we know. Have any of you been asked, over the past year or so, about black, floating shadow like things?"

Jill Rafferity was sitting in back and was over hearing the pastors discussion, *oh my gosh she thought I'm not the only one who has seen those things. Maybe I am sane!* She got up and began walking out to the pastors to find out more. She heard Pastor Paulson bursting out in laugher. She stiffened and returned to her seat. *"Maybe I can just talk with that pastor Hayes he really seems to know."*

Pastor Paulson continued on, "As a matter of fact, yes. What surprised me is that they came from some of our most respected members."

Father O'Hara, surprised, replied, "What? You don't believe in demons?"

Pastor Paulson chuckled again. "I think we can agree that we make our own demons.

Pastor Hayes glanced wearily at Paulson and replied, "Gentlemen, I can tell you about thousands of these reports coming in from all around the world. At Christ's Sword church eighty percent of my congregation has come to me claiming to have seen these things. As a matter of fact, humbly and respectfully, so have I." The three pastors just sat there not knowing what to say.

"Why can't we then Pastor?" replied Paulson.

Hayes responded somberly, "I know we have our differences when it comes to the Holy Spirit! But in the Book of Acts 1:14, The Bible tells us of an experience unlike any other that took place in an upper room. It also tells us that it's for anyone who truly wants it, just read Acts 2:38. I believe that God has opened the eyes of everyone who has received the Holy Spirit."

"I know that he guides us," Pastor Adams added, "but to think he lives in us? What about our freedom of choice?"

Pastor Hayes, realizing that they didn't understand and it was getting late, decided on a different approach. He looked at the other three warmly. "Would you be willing to try something?" They sat back feeling very uncomfortable, but willing.

"What?" asked Father O'Hara.

"Loving God means having a relationship with him everyday. Taking time to pray and read his word. Would you come to Christ's Sword one night this week and pray? Just pray that's all I ask!" They all agreed. Shaking hands, they parted company.

"Did you really mean all that stuff you just spoke of?"

"Who's out there?" called Hayes. Jill Rafferity walked out toward Pastor Hayes. "I'm sorry Pastor Hayes. I couldn't help but over hear you." Then she asked him again, "Did you really mean all that stuff?"

Hayes had a huge smile across his face, he could see the hand of God working right before him and it was glorious.

"Yes, my dear, I meant every word. Tell me, do you see the dark creatures as well. Hesitantly Jill took time to think before responding. "Does that mean I have that Holy Spirit you were talking about?"

"Ms. Rafferity, I believe somewhere in your life you reached out for the hand of God and he came. I don't know when, only you would know that, think back."

Jill began to remember when her grandmother was near death. The town she grew up in was very small and help just wasn't available. It was possible that she was just to young to know what to do. I do remember that she died. I remember begging and begging God for help. "Where was he? My grandmother was all I had!" she replied as tears began to form in her eyes.

Hayes just smiled. "My child, he was right where he was when his son died. Only this time he was next to your Grandmother.

Taking her hand in his, he continued, "Sometimes he helps in ways we don't expect and that's when faith comes in. While he helped your grandmother, he comforted you with his spirit. It's a great and wonderful gift, given freely. Jill, Jesus loves you very much."

Jill Rafferity stood wiping away the tears in her eyes and provided a soft kiss on the Pastor's cheek. Then, without another word, quietly left the room.

Sitting alone, pondering what God had just done, Pastor Hayes was confident he knew his God wouldn't let him down. *This week he thought to himself with a big smile, three more men are going to get the Holy Ghost! Suddenly a quick thought flashed through his mind, "I wonder, maybe I can speak to them about water Baptism as well?"*

CHAPTER 21

"Welcome gentlemen to Christ's Sword. Please come in."

Pastors Paulson, Adams and Jaspers followed Pastor Hayes into the tabernacle.

"New ushers!" replied Pastor Adams with his usual sense of humor.

Pastor Jaspers took a few minutes to look around before joining the others. "You don't believe in decorating around here, do you Hayes?" There were no stain glass windows or pictures of Jesus with long hair. The walls though had beautiful solid wood paneling with crystal chandeliers placed in rows of four, providing a beautiful, gentle glow that fell upon the pews beneath them. The building was quaint, small in comparison to the other church buildings in the area. There was something different about it that Jaspers just couldn't put his finger on.

"Are you coming?" called Hayes. The pastor stood there in front of the church, only this time there was something different about him. Tonight he seemed powerful, displaying a certain kind of boldness that drew attention immediately.

Feeling a little embarrassed, Jaspers hurried to catch up to the rest.

"Gentlemen, I see that you all came prepared. Each man brought in something to share with the others. Jaspers was carrying a cooler containing soft drinks, Paulson had a bag of sandwiches, and Pastor Adams was in a humorous mood that evening. He brought in one small bag of mints which, when he took them out of the bag, were already half eaten. This created a huge round of laughter among the four, breaking the ice and creating a wonderful bond. Everything that Hayes had been praying for.

Pastor Hayes walked over and took Adams' mints away. "I'll save these for later, after all, these mints are such a temptation!"

Pastor Hayes removed the refreshments from the area. As he did, Pastors Paulson, Adams and Jaspers began a very serious discussion between themselves. "Have you seen the news lately? Now they are calling us terrorists! Can you believe it?"

"Yes." replied Adams. "I was watching those late night talk shows and they are actually encouraging our friends and neighbors to join in the fight against certain Christian groups."

"You mean the groups speaking out against homosexuality and gay marriage?" Hollywood is doing they're very best to promote the subject as something innocent. Movies, even ones for children, are promoting it."

"I have been asking my parishioners to try not to watch television at all, but to some it's all the social interaction they get other than coming to church! How can I fault them for that?"

Pastor Hayes overheard the conversation and interrupted them. "Gentlemen, I believe that people today have lost sight of what sin is. Television and movies are embracing sin with out knowing what they are doing or they simply have become numb and don't care anymore. I'm sorry if I interrupted you, but it is a big topic these day's. No matter what church you belong to, I truly believe that with all this humanistic psychology placed within our social circle, and the huge liberal presence spreading their pseudo logic, God is slowly being taking out of our society. I'm concerned people no longer fear God!"

The four Pastors sat quiet for a few minutes thinking about what pastor Hayes had just said.

"Last night I was watching the Gene Mar Show" replied Jaspers, "I truly believe we need to address this problem within our respective congregations."

"Was the show that bad?" replied Adams.

"Seriously many within my congregation believe that the young people accused of those murders actually killed those doctors! The media has already tried and convicted the young woman!"

"Remind you of anyone?" replied Pastor Hayes.

Jaspers only provided a weak smile then replied, "I thank God those two senators were there to witness what actually happened! Nathanial, what about that young women?" Not willing to provide information to these men about the plan, at least not until he was sure where they stood, Pastor Hayes decided to settle on just providing her name. "I'll give her name to you with absolute confidence of her innocence, "therefore, Her name is Esther James, replied Hayes.

"Two of the people that were taken came from your church, why is that?" asked Jaspers. "That can't be a coincidence!"

Pastor Hayes stood to his feet then turned his back to the other three.

"Like we discussed at the auditorium, we are fighting more then just those two men in that high office. That's all I can say until later." Adams stood and offered a comforting hand to Pastor Hayes. "I understand how you must feel Hayes, the young man in our church is Larry Bates."

"He has a wife and a daughter and believe me they are upset. Our church has hired an attorney for him; I'm confidant that he will be back home soon."

All Pastor Hayes could do was to think about Esther and his concern for her. He had been holding onto it for so long that it began to build, then suddenly, deep from within arose a mighty shout, "I know that Esther is safe and I trust in God to keep her that way! Hayes stood there in shock. Did that really come out of him? Shock turned to embarrassment and his face developed a bright red color. The three pastors proceeded to break out in laughter.

"Feel better?" asked Paulson. "Tell me Hayes, what is going on here at this church?"

Hayes looked at him inquisitively, "What do you mean?"

"We have noticed what seems to be a small army of young people arriving into this area. *I might say, mainly to your church!* "What's up?"

"After tonight. God willing, all will be explained to you.

I asked you here tonight for prayer. Lets not argue about things that can't be discussed anyhow! If you agree, then let's begin." Together the four men shifted their bodies and fell to their knees. Pastor Hayes began by reciting biblical scripture as to why receiving the Holy Spirit was so important. "Friends, in the book of Acts Chapter 10, the whole chapter tells the story about a man named Cornelius. He was a devoted man that feared God! But something was missing; something so important that God sent Peter to him, why? So that he and his house could receive the Holy Spirit!"

It is obvious, that if God found it important for Cornelius, who by the way was a gentile. It's important for us as well."

Now let's look in the book of Romans Chapter 8, the whole Chapter describes the very importance of receiving it and then living by it."

Adams looked up at him respectfully, "I know we need the Holy Spirit, but to believe that he actually lives in us? We believe him to be more of a guide."

"He is our guide!" replied Hayes. Lifting his bible he began reading. "In the book of Acts Chapter 1: 12-14, it reads, about an upper room. Where everyone, yes, even Jesus' mother Mary, had gathered to pray. They were waiting on the comforter to arrive. When the comforter arrived in Acts 2:1-4, what did everyone do? They all spoke in tongues. Tongues had been given not only as a sign to whom ever received it, but also as a sign too those that didn't believe. "Can anyone here provide any scripture, anywhere, describing where someone received the Holy Spirit without speaking in tongues?"

"O.K! Pastor, let's begin already!" replied Paulson. "My knees are beginning to fall asleep."

"Open your hearts tonight. If we do our part tonight, God will do His!"

Soon all four men were embraced in a loud conversation with God. Loud moans could be heard across the building, and Pastor Hayes could feel the Holy Ghost all around them. In a small way, now more than ever he wished there were more of those listening devices around, maybe the guy's on the other end could pick up on a little Jesus! Now wouldn't that be something! He thought with a smile.

He got up and moved over to Pastor Adams and placed his hand on the back of his head. After a while Adams began to quiver and his hands began to shake. Sitting back on his knees, tears were streaming down his face. Adam's could feel a warm sensation cover his body, then his lips began quivering rapidly, Pastor Hayes knew it was time and quietly whispered in his ear, "Now just let him in." Pastor Adams opened his mouth and strange words began flowing out.

God was giving Pastor Adams his gift so Pastor Hayes stood and went to the next person helping each Pastor. He stayed sensitive to the spirit, trying to be an instrument of God never attempting to push. Pastor Hayes waited until all three men were filled with the true baptism of the Holy Spirit. All the men were weeping and speaking in tongues. This went on for three more hours until they finally collapsed.

"I don't believe what I have missed all these years." replied Paulson sobbing. "I never really believed it was real!"

Pastor Adams leaned over and placed his face in his hands and wept! "This is going to change everything for my family and me! I don't know how my congregation is going to react to this!"

Jaspers stood to his feet and embraced Pastor Hayes, "Thank you for helping me to open my eyes Pastor."

Hayes took time and just talked to the three as to what had just taken place. Then, took them back to his living quarters for the sandwiches and soft drinks that the three Pastors brought in earlier and of course that half a bag of mints that Adams brought. They certainly didn't want to miss out on that treat. While they were eating Jaspers asked, "You said all would be explained tonight! Please elaborate!"

Pastor Hayes looked at the three with a huge smile across his face, the greatest miracle already had taken place, but, yes, there was more.

"You have the Holy Spirit living inside you just as he promised! Now I can call you brothers. Do you remember our discussion concerning those floating dark shadow creatures?" While discussing the matter, Pastor Hayes switched on his television set and DVD player. "Here is video from news footage from four years ago when President McChellan arrived for the first time at the Whitehouse! "Watch closely." The four men watched as McChellan stepped out of his limousine. For the first time, the three Pastors sat in astonishment, McChellan had something dark climbing all over him, and they saw it for themselves.

Paulson cried out "My Lord, forgive me!" Pastor Hayes reached out to him. "It's all right my brother. Blinded eyes are now opened. Your eyes are opened to the truth. Jesus understands that."

Paulson pulled away. "I know he forgives, but I'm finding it hard to forgive myself. All the people that looked to me for guidance, I feel as if I let them down. That creature! Is he who I think he is? Are we really in the last days that are spoken of in the bible?"

All three men were distraught at what they saw except Hayes. "Pastors calm yourselves, this is not the devil, but subjects of his, doing his bidding. We must remember that the devil is not omnipresent. He can't be everywhere. Look at how many creatures there are. Do you recall in mark 5: 1-9, the book tells us how after Jesus and his disciples crossed the sea; they came across a man possessed with unclean spirits. Did you notice the bible said, *spirits*, meaning more then one! This man was so bad that the people attempted to chain him but the chains wouldn't hold. He was so strong the bible says no man could tame him. The man was in such torment that he cut himself day and night. When he saw our Lord coming to him, he fell to his knees and worshiped him, pleading with him not to torment him. Then with a loud voice the man cried out, son of the most high what have I to do with thee, and once again pleaded for mercy. Brethren, when Jesus asked him his name, the voice that came from within the man answered, *my name is legion for we are many*. My brothers, the devil has many helping him. They are what we are really fighting, not the man, President McChellan."

"I believe, we are in the last days and our Lord will be coming soon. I expect we will see more of this thing in the future. We see this evil everyday of our lives only at a smaller level. Everytime we see greed or hear about killings, this is the same evil we have just seen on that screen. When someone kills another person, we need to pray for that person as much as the person who just lost their life, because it's not him that's doing the killing, but the evil creature within man! I'm not saying that he or she should not be held accountable for their actions but, perhaps, with a little more understanding of the truth, we might be able to love our enemies a little easier.

Brethren, this same evil has gained control over our government. The most powerful office in the free world has grown so powerful that, I believe, God has decided to let us see it for what it is. Maybe it's our wake up call, I don't know, but I know this, that he's counting on us to listen carefully to him and follow his directions at any cost. I believe we all know with God all things are possible!"

"One final thought that comes to mind. In the book of Ephesians 6: 12, It says that we wrestle not against flesh and blood but against principalities, against powers, against the rulers of darkness of this world, against spiritual wickedness in high places! Sound familiar?"

The three pastors sat back. The intensity of their thoughts was etched deeply in the furrows of their eyebrows.

"I never thought I'd see this day!" exclaimed Jaspers, "What now?"

Hayes walked over to his desk and brought back a long list of names.

"Those young people you spoke of before, well, they are coming in from overseas. Our organization brought them in from outside the country. They are part of His plan! Yes, Pastors, we have a plan and another phase is about to begin. A letter has been sent, and the one that's required is coming, pray for her safety. I know that our enemy is ready, by using unrecognizable faces. It gives us time to finish our tasks before they catch on, and with God's guidance, He will give us the victory!"

CHAPTER 22

At last, BBS News reporter Shelly Cleveland arrived at her destination and was quite fatigued from her long journey. Shelly pulled up in front of an old country farmhouse. There she sat for a few minutes trying to wake up. The trip had been very long, to have traveled all at one time. However, the worse part was that she needed to return immediately, leaving her no time for rest.

Gently, she laid her head back and closed her eyes but only for a minute not knowing who could be watching. Reaching into her slightly larger than normal stack of "to-do-stuff," she removed a medium sized brown colored envelope; one she received from Pastor Hayes. Holding up the letter, she checked over the address one more time just to make sure she hadn't made an error finding the location.

Shelly had just completed a five-hour drive from D.C. into Crystal City, a quant farming town. She was fatigued and really wanted something to drink. Hopefully, these people were kind and had something cold.

Exiting her vehicle, she began walking up to the door. Shelly stopped for a moment to feel the wind blowing through her hair. It felt so warm and soothing.

She noticed how nice the countryside looked, the open grass fields seemed to sway with the wind as if in tune with some kind of heavenly music. The colors of the sky were painted so skillfully! And the flowers this homeowner grew amazed her. They were so well organized. Their aroma could almost place you into a trance.

"God really does good work!" she thought to herself. Shelly only came here because Pastor Hayes asked a favor. She didn't know what was in the letter or why they needed it in a hurry, only that the Pastor needed her help and after all he had done for her, she felt honored in a weird way.

Knocking on the door she wondered what she was walking into. Favor or not, this whole thing seemed rather odd. The house was beautiful. The outside consisted of huge bay windows, surrounded by burnt-brown colored bricks. Underneath the window sat two large flower boxes filled with a mixture of different types of plants and flowers. On the side of the house they placed a huge fireplace that completely distinguished the home with a unique style. Cobblestone was used for the sidewalk that led to a huge wooden front door, surrounded by a solid wrought iron rail used for hand support.

Slowly the door opened and middle-aged women poked her head out from the corner of the door.

"Yes, she asked timidly."

"Hello my name is Shelly Cleveland."

The woman just stood there looking at her with a hint of concern on her face. Reaching in her purse Shelly pulled out her BBS identification badge.

"You're a reporter?" asked the women. Before Shelly could utter another word the woman began closing the door on her, but her reporter skills kicked in as she managed to place one foot in the doorway keeping it ajar.

"I thought that Pastor Hayes had informed you that I would be arriving today?"

"Pastor Hayes sent you?" She gasped while struggling to close the door. Her voice sounded alarming and yet at the same time relieved. Shelly could tell by the sound in her voice that the stress level was slowly being removed from between them, but why was she so frightened?

The woman stepped back and opened the door.

"Please forgive me, welcome to my home," the woman replied.

As Shelly entered the home she noticed the beautiful paintings that hung from the walls all around the room. The smell of fresh baked apple pie filled the air intoxicating her senses. She just stood there with her eyes closed taking it all in. "I think I died and went to heaven!" She spoke in a soft whisper. Then from a distance two voices began to laugh instead of one.

There standing in the door way stood Esther James holding a slice of that pie covered with vanilla ice cream.

The unknown woman approached Shelly and held out her hand, "I'm sorry Ms. Cleveland I do remember you now. How is Tom?" She asked with a playful smile, "He is a funny man when he gets nervous!" Shelly looked at her carefully. She knew Tom? Then all at once Shelly recognized her and both she and Fran broke out in laughter, remembering their discussion at the coffee shop.

"It's nice to see you again Fran." It was Fran Staples the same women who brought her all the accounting documents from Aztec motors!

Shelly walked over and gave her a huge hug.

"I'm so sorry I couldn't get back to you, but a lot of unexpected things have happened. The papers you gave me, I gave to my boss, who as it turned out provided them to the bad guys, so I believe my days as a reporter are numbered."

"Shelly, I made other copies, I know that Pastor Hayes has a copy as well as Senator Morrison. I'm sure they will make good use of them."

"That's a relief, I thought I really blew it this time."

"Esther, do you think I can get a slice of that pie? It smells heavenly and maybe a soft drink? The drive here was longer then I thought."

Soon all three women adjourned to the patio in the back of the house.

"So you're the young women all of D.C. wants!"

Esther's smile dissolved and an expression of sadness took its place.

"Yes, but I didn't do anything! I was just sitting next to my mother, then the next thing I knew they were all pointing toward me making outlandish accusations, I was so frightened,"

"Fran, do realize the risks you are taking?"

"Look Ms. Cleveland, there is something going on in D.C. that's wrong! There are just to many odd things happening within the system. I want to help if it rids our country of this evil. I want to do my part! Besides, look at her, where would she have gone? Does she look like someone who would walk into an abortion clinic and kill anyone?"

Placing her fork onto her plate Shelly sat quietly for a moment, then she smiled. You couldn't have chosen a better place to stay. Reaching into her purse she pulled out an envelope and handed it to Fran. "I drove out here as a favor to Pastor Hayes! He wanted me to deliver this to you, I guess he didn't trust the mail."

Fran excused herself and went into the house to read the letter. "You really made quite the fuss out there."

"It seems to happened to me quite often lately, I wish it would stop."

"Esther I'm not going to ask you for your story right now, you have enough to worry about, but when this is over, do you think I can have the exclusive story?"

"I would like that Shelly."

Just then Fran returned with the letter in hand, "ladies I'm afraid I'll need to cut this short. Shelly, I hope you will come out again and pay a visit when we can talk about better things."

"I would really like that! exclaimed Shelly, "was it bad news?" "I'm sorry that I can't elaborate, but let's just say a plan is now in action and if you really want a great story be at the Whitehouse grounds on voting day."

Esther rose from her seat. "It's begun?" she was all at once exhilarated and apprehensive.

Fran just nodded her head and smiled. Esther knew the answer was yes!

Esther let loose with a shout that could be heard throughout the valley, then walked over and gave a huge hug to Shelly, almost knocking her to the ground.

"WOW! What was that?" She asked laughing, while trying to regain her balance.

"You will find out soon enough!" replied Fran. "Please tell Pastor Hayes hello from us and thank you for his message."

The two women walked to the front of the house where Shelly's car was parked. "Please, Shelly, come back and visit when all this is over. I'd like to be friends! Right now things are going to get worse before they get better."

"I'm glad that I could help. Pastor Hayes has been wonderful to me. He has helped my career immensely. This little thing is the least I could do for him and, after meeting Esther, I know many good people believe in her and, personally, so do I."

CHAPTER 23

Early morning in D.C. was as most other cities in America but today was special. It was Election Day!

Barney Klein a long time friend of Clint and Mary James was volunteering his truck to deliver some boxes to the church.

Down the street he came rumbling in an old white laundry truck. The truck was not much to look at. Rust covered the wheel wells and the engine was badly in need of a tune up. Slowing down he pulled into the church parking lot, stopping for a moment to check his manifest before proceeding toward the back of the building.

The lights were not on yet, so he decided to finish his coffee. Without warning, four black sedans raced into the parking lot and surround his truck!

Barney sat up quickly, spilling his coffee across his lap. Frantically, he began wiping the spilled coffee from his lap all the while filling the air with colorful metaphors directed toward the men that were surrounding his truck, and what nerve, at this time of the morning yet.

Barney rolled down his window and leaned out wondering what was going on. Four men dressed in black approached his truck, then divided into two groups each moving to either side of the truck. Two men on the driver's side pulled open the door and forcefully pulled old Barney from the truck causing him to hit his head on the concrete.

Never indentifying themselves, the men held Barney down. One of them placed his knee directly on the middle of his neck while the other grabbed his hands and cuffed him from behind. Barney fought in vain to get away, but these men were powerful. Their grip seemed to get tighter the more he struggled.

After cuffing him, one of the men left and joined the other two who had opened the trailer of his truck.

The men began removing the boxes and threw them to the ground not caring if anything broke. Barney made one last effort to tell them that they were just hooded sweatshirts with the church name printed on the front, but the men went on until they were satisfied.

The three men stood at the end of the truck discussing something but they were too far away from Barney for him to hear anything clearly. He knew they were angry about something by the way they were acting.

The sun began to rise now and the men walked back toward Barney. The man holding Barney down released the cuffs from his wrists and helped Barney up.

"If you had just asked me what in the world you were looking for, maybe I could have helped! Look at all the mess I have to clean up!"

The men just ignored him and returned to their cars and then left, leaving as they came, in a great hurry. Barney dusted himself off and walked to the back of the trailer to examine the damage. Barney's self-esteem was already at an all time low, and this certainly didn't help.

"*How is Pastor Hayes going to understand this? I was trusted to perform this simple task and I couldn't even do this right!*" Hearing the footsteps, Barney turned to see the subject of his thoughts rushing toward him.

"Are you alright?"

Barney stood with his hands raised in a gesture of surrender toward the Pastor wondering why this happened.

"Pastor, they did all this for some sweatshirts?"

"I'm sorry, Barney, I should have warned you. I couldn't tell you the real reason for this delivery, the hoodies are important but this is far more valuable!"

Climbing in the back of the trailer, Pastor Hayes walked toward the front of the truck and began knocking on the steel wall. Barney stood there scratching his head wondering just what was going on? Pastor Hayes gave a little chuckle and then revealed the real package.

The rear wall began to separate itself from the sidewalls and a small compartment came into view.

Esther James and Fran Staples slowly began climbing out of the small compartment and began stretching their limbs from being in the cramped area they had to hide in for so many hours.

Barney never knew the two women were hidden inside his truck and, because he didn't know, he accidently chose other deliveries before coming to Christ's Sword, causing him to finish other deliveries first, increasing the amount of hours they needed to occupy that small area!

"That was too close Pastor." Fran replied while rubbing her legs trying to regain circulation back into them.

"I'm just glad that Shelly made it out to deliver my message. Go on in and make yourselves comfortable, your rooms are ready!"

Barney walked over to Pastor Hayes with a bit of a chip on his shoulder. "Why didn't you tell me what was going on? Maybe I could have come in a different way or perhaps even came here first."

Pastor Hayes understood Barney's anxiety; after all, he was used in a way that got him physically harmed.

"Listen Barney, I'm very sorry we had to do it this way but it was for your protection as much as for theirs. We needed to make it look as real as possible in order to fool them. I'm not sure that you would have reacted as you did if you had known what was going on. We knew that they would want to search every vehicle that came into this place, especially today. I'm very sorry you got hurt!"

Barney walked over to Esther and gave her a big hug. "Maybe next time they will trust me enough to tell me, then perhaps I could of missed a few of those pot holes I hit."

Both Esther and Fran grabbed their bags and hurried to the church building. Barney and Pastor Hayes began picking up the sweatshirts and repacking them in the broken boxes.

"Why is she here Pastor? What's with all these hooded sweatshirts? Are you having a concert or something?"

Pastor Hayes provided an inquisitive look, then a slight smile. "Barney, soon you will find that out! But for now lets finish this up and get some rest. Today is a big day for this nation and us, it is voting day!"

CHAPTER 24

The inner city was awakened by the sight and sound of bright yellow school buses. Columns of the bright shinny vehicles roared though the streets toward preplanned destinations. Hundreds of young people were being dropped off throughout the city.

Separating into groups of two, they scattered into the poorer neighborhoods praying for whoever would accept their invitations, concentrating mainly on the homeless and the elderly. They taught on salvation every chance they got, but today they also taught a mixed message.

First, they brought the message of Christ's death, burial and resurrection, and the importance of water baptism. Second, they taught about the Holy Ghost and Christ's return. Then they changed the topic all together, speaking about the challenges that lay ahead for the nation, and the men God sent to lead them out of it. Finally, they spoke about the government as a whole and the difficulties the administration had placed upon the people, adding what they could do as citizens to help put an end to the atrocities.

Pastors Hayes and Adams organized the northern and southern areas of town, while Pastors Jaspers and Paulson organized the eastern and western parts of town.

"This should put a little starch in their collars this morning, we need to brace ourselves for any repercussions. I know they won't take this lightly." replied Adams!

This indeed began creating quite a stir in the Whitehouse.

President McChellan, along with Vice President Marcus Holland and Sam Hill, McChellan's campaign manager, gathered in the oval office to observe the results as they came in.

"We ran a great campaign Mr. President", "I feel confident!"

"With all the new tax cuts in the works, I'm sure that this will persuade most of the people out there to vote our way. After all, we have become their heroes. We're the ones who made it possible for them to keep their businesses afloat. The larger companies perhaps most of all.

Marcus Holland was feeling pretty agitated about how things were really adding up, after all, they were counting on a land slide victory and it was far from it. He knew something was wrong, but this blasted campaign seemed to occupy too much of his mind to really put his finger on it.

Their latest rating losses over the last few days had been dismal.

He just received reports from downtown regarding attacks on their reputations from, of all people, a bunch of young Jesus freaks. To Marcus, it wasn't the kids that worried him, but the stir they were creating within the city. Needless to say, he was more than just a little less than convinced of Mr. Hill's words.

"Let's examine this a little closer. Lester you dropped 25% in the recent popularity poll. Many people out there are saying they can't trust you to keep your word, yet good old Sam here sits back and says everything is fine."

"But is it?"

"Are you aware that as many as five hundred young people took to the streets this morning! Our next generation of voters is out there speaking against us! And Lester, from our intelligence sources, I can tell you that many people are listening." "if you know my meaning."

"You can't be serious!" gasped Hill. "You actually believe that a little prayer here and there is going to influence the people enough to win this election? The people from those sections of town understand only two things Mr. Vice President. First, where will they get their next bottle from, and then second, where will they find a place to sleep that's safe."

"Seems we have helped everyone but them!" scoffed Holland. McChellan listened carefully to both men, unfortunately for Sam. He began looking very weak in the President's eyes. While Hill spoke, McChellan didn't hear a word coming from the man's mouth. Instead, his mind shifted and focused on the mistakes he's made during this election, this one was perhaps the biggest blunder of them all.

He used Hill much the same way he used Jill Rafferity. The creature never turned Sam Hill, His thinking was that because he, himself, could not feel compassion or sincerity, he needed someone who could write the words that hit home. The words that made people feel good about his plans and instill the peoples' trust. This left him vulnerable to something he hadn't expected. The demon inside McChellan knew something was amiss. Just as Holland, he couldn't concentrate. His mind was being bombarded with thoughts not typical of himself. McChellan was once able to think outside the box, keeping him in touch with everyone and every place his influence was, but not any longer. McChellan was being limited in his thinking, perhaps making him vulnerable. The image of Esther James kept popping up in his mind. For some reason he began to worry less about the election and more on making sure that this young woman was far away from him. The creature in him knew she was dangerous to him somehow, but he still didn't understand how!

Now one thing had to be addressed he thought, for now, it was Sam Hill. Perhaps Mr. Hill was seeing him for what he was, perhaps not a demon in reality, but someone much like himself, maybe, worse. Perhaps Hill was actually working for his enemy, the one who was causing such a problem outside on the eastern grounds. Paranoia overwhelmed him, now, more then ever. McChellan wanted this man gone, for good.

"Alright Mr. Hill, tell me, what do you think is going to help us in these districts?" snapped McChellan, the tone in his voice left Sam Hill just a little worried. Sam knew whatever he said had better sound convincing.

"After we cut the entertainment taxes across the board, alcohol and cigarettes will be made more affordable, isn't that what drunks and losers really care about anyhow?"

"Give them what they want!"

This angered Holland even more. He grabbed Hill by the front of his shirt. Holland was now standing face to face with Sam Hill.

"Mr. Hill, those young people out there on the streets are doing more then, as you say preach a few words here and there. These kids are bringing hope. You don't know my adversary very well. He brings hope; that's one thing we don't want them to have."

"Tell me Marcus, what can we do to stop them? Is it to late to do anything meaningful?"

Sam Hill collected himself the best he could, he wanted out as this Presidents advisor as soon as possible. He knew the only way this nightmare was going to end was to play along for as long as he was able, and then run. Hill reluctantly interrupted their conversation.

"Lester, many people out there believe that these young people are a cult and won't listen to them. Many of the upper middle class are working again and for them life is better. I believe they recognize this and are giving you the credit. I'm confident of their vote!"

Marcus couldn't believe it, but Sam Hill actually did him a favor by giving him a wonderful idea to put a dent in the Christian's strategy.

"Lester lets use the media to our advantage. I can have some of the youth arrested."

"Marcus, the people out there aren't stupid."

"Lester, allow me to finish! Think of how the public would respond if they saw some of these kids in the act of committing an assault on the homeless. We can set it up so that the police arrive just in time to save the day. That should make them look pretty bad to all those bleeding hearts! And, of course, I can make sure that we have major media coverage there on the spot at the time of the arrests. You know the media, once they have their hands on a story, true or not, they cover it until it dies, which could last for weeks. Our goal here, Lester, is to have our adversary look bad to the public. Another thought that came to mind was to do something with the camera imaging, and hopefully, trick the people into believing that these people are violent and not to be taken seriously but, Lester, we need to do this before the polls close today."

"I have another concern Marcus. They're up to something. I can feel it!"

"I know, Lester, I've been watching them from my office. It seems the number of people out there has grown considerably."

Indeed it was. Outside on the eastern side of the Whitehouse grounds, the group that once began with a handful of youth from Christ's Sword, now numbered more than one thousand.

"Don't worry too much Lester. They're probably just wanting good spots for our victory celebration" replied Hill.

"Mr. Hill, Marcus was right, you are taking our enemy for granted."

Sam Hill felt the skin on the back of his neck crawl. It just dawned on him just how stupid his last comment was, and the timing couldn't have been worse. While Holland and McChellan planned the demise of the Christians, he decided to break away before more trouble could come his way. McChellan's last words seemed to bother Hill, all this talk about an enemy, "*What enemy were they referring to?*" Sam was becoming more convinced that these guy's were nuts and he needed to get out. Reaching the outer hall, he stopped and looked down the corridor for any secret service standing guard or anyone who could tell McChellan what he was about to do.

No phone calls were to be made around the oval office without the President's consent. He wanted to make sure he was alone before removing his cell phone from his jacket pocket. Dialing the number, he waited for what seemed an eternity, finally someone answered.

"It's me, listen, all I can say is watch out. They are planning something and soon. Plan on bad press." He quickly hung up, *"Ooh that Jill, what she doesn't make me do."*

The sound of footsteps approached from down the hall. They were coming fast, sending Sam twisting like a pretzel while he tried to get his phone back into his pocket. Quickly standing to attention, Sam quickly lit up a cigarette as not to attract attention. Fred Joiner hurried past him as if he wasn't even there, going straight into the oval office. The cigarette fell from Sam's lips from sheer nervousness. Slowly, he removed his handkerchief and wiped his brow, Hill knew what would have happened if he would have been caught. Loud voices emerged from within McChellan's office.

"Mr. President, I have the latest numbers. I'm sorry to say, so far it's pretty close."

"Out of the remaining six states that are yet to close, Senator Morrison holds the lead in Texas, Wyoming, and Wisconsin; you lead in the three remaining states. I'm sorry to say Mr. President that it's to close to tell right now!"

Sam realized his days were numbered and he couldn't be happier. Hurrying to his office, he took what papers he had involving the campaign and departed by the nearest staircase.

In the oval office, McChellan sat in his chair with a wet cloth draped over his eyes. The creature within him was stirring. So much was on the line and too much could go wrong. He was frustrated and overwhelmed by this election. He wanted to have won this election by a landslide but now that was not to be. What was worse, he knew that his adversary was nearby.

Pulling the wet cloth from his eyes. McChellan looked up at Fred with disappointment in his eyes.

"Alright Fred! I know that you haven't apprehended her yet, have you!

Trembling Fred stood fumbling with his papers trying desperately to find the right words to say. "No sir. We still can't locate her."

"That's because he's hiding her Fred. Do I have to reiterate the importance of finding her?" Find her at any cost!"

Then with a stare that could intimidate even the darkest of souls, he uttered, "Do you understand?

Fred hurried from the room leaving the President and Vice President alone.

"The James girl?" replied Holland.

"Yes, Marcus. We need to find her and soon!"

Newscasts began appearing on every television screen across America. Who were these young kids invading D.C.? Reports were being circulated all around the city about the different groups of young people roaming the streets and their connection to the group gathered at the Whitehouse. Some say they were there to make a statement, others warned of possible terrorism and suggested the government take immediate action. Hollywood took their cue as well. Show's like "The Gene Marr Show" began getting into the scene giving Esther James and Clarence Banks celebrity status. They created stories about their family lives and their possible connection with this strange group of young people.

Shelly and her cameraman, Tom, arrived at the Whitehouse early afternoon, waiting for what she was told, will be the story of all stories. She knew the story everyone else was chasing was a bust. These kids wouldn't hurt a flea, so why would they attack homeless people who were helpless to defend themselves? Shelly knew Esther James and she knew those kids were harmless. *No, for once, no matter what the producer thought, I'll stick to the real story!"*

"Set-up over by that statue Tom. We will camp there until whatever that's suppose to go down does."

"What will go down?"

"I don't know yet but by the way Esther was acting, I know it's going to be big."

CHAPTER 25

Senators Morrison and Peeling watched the results with family and friends.

"I can't believe we have come this far!" exclaimed Peeling. He was excited as a schoolboy, prancing around the room, giving high fives to anyone he came in contact with.

"We still have three hours before the polls close. We didn't win yet!" replied Morrison.

"No, but I never dreamed that we would ever be this close. Look at the screen! We're ahead!"

It was true. After everything that the administration attempted to do to corrupt the election, it had come down to what would happen in the remaining two states.

Morrison kept his eye on the television screen, not totally believing what he saw. He glanced over toward his campaign manager, Ross Cortland, and asked, "How could this be happening?"

Ross was sitting in a big rocking chair enjoying his favorite cigar, sipping a cool glass of lemon aid.

"As I see it William, not just anyone can register a vote. All those who hadn't voted yet in the central states are out of luck. The polls are now closed in those states.

Since we went to a new election process, voting has become easier, not better, just simpler!"

"We know that it's down to only two states. I would be naive to think that the President doesn't have his hounds out looking for a way to destroy us!" replied Peeling.

McChellan was furious. How could this be happening? All their plans were going up in smoke and he felt helpless to prevent it.

"Fred, get me Justice Lasitor on the phone! I need answers! What happened to all the promises that were made to me! How did this happen?"

The creature within him could sense he was losing control. His power to manipulate people was lessening, making him vulnerable to his real human emotions. "Fred did you find that women yet?"

Fred hurried into the oval office with a sandwich in his mouth and notepad in hand.

"Sir, I believe she's being hidden at her church. I know her pastor. He's bold enough to do just about anything!"

"Enough! I don't care how, just get her!"

Fred dropped his notepad on the office floor and ran back to his desk. He knew that he had to come through for McChellan but, for some reason, it was proving to be more difficult this time. Fred was in a war and the battle was coming from deep within. The creature within Fred was weakening. From time to time memories of who he once was would surface in his mind. In the end, however, Fred gave in and placed the telephone calls that could get his friend, Esther James, in serious trouble.

At Christ's Sword Church, the four black sedans parked on the street had their orders. One by one they left their posts and approached the building from different angles. Their goal was to block every exit, attempting to cover every possible means of escape.

Pastor Hayes was just finishing a telephone conversation when Esther and Fran hurried into his office.

"Pastor they're here!" they explained trembling.

Pastor Hayes noticed the fear in Esther's eyes. By the sound of the squeak in her voice, he knew that the anxiety she was feeling was real. Calmly he placed his hand on her shoulder and drew her in close and whispered softly, "Now is your time Esther. Remember, this is God's plan so it can't fail! He will keep you safe."

The three sat in his office and prayed for a while gaining strength for what was about to happen. After making sure they felt prepared, he guided them into a spare room so she could prepare.

Pastor Hayes left the two and walked into the church tabernacle to address a crowd of young people that were waiting for their instructions. "Don't worry about those men outside. They cannot enter into this building unless invited! We must move fast. Your hoodies are in those boxes on the table. Please help yourselves to one and make yourselves ready. Timing is everything, if this is going to work!"

Outside two large yellow school buses arrived. The agents rushed into the buses and began searching for anything unusual or out of place but found nothing.

Inside the church, the young people hurried over to Fran who distributed the sweatshirts. Fran was frightened. Pastor Hayes knew this could mean real trouble for her if anything went wrong. He tried his best to reassure her that everything was in God's hands. Fran was new to knowing God and her faith was weak. Uncertainty filled her mind, clouding her senses and making it difficult to concentrate. At the same time, she felt a strange peace in her heart. She didn't know if she should trust it and yet, this peace didn't come from Pastor's words.

"Are you ready for this?" he asked her tenderly.

"Yes Pastor, but I truly wish this was over with!"

Pastor Hayes knew Fran's capabilities. If she was bold enough to get those files from Aztec, surely, she could do this.

Again Pastor Hayes addressed all the youth standing in the tabernacle. "Once you have your sweatshirts, exit the building and enter your assigned bus as fast as you can, please hurry!"

Outside, the FBI agents were pounding on the church door trying to gain entry, never expecting the great hoard that exploded toward them. The doors opened fast and with great force, pushing one agent to the ground. The young people began pushing their way through the agents, attempting to reach their assigned bus. The agents frantically tried to grab each person, pulling back their hoods, checking for their identities.

After the bus was full, two of the agents climbed on board and rechecked every person, to make sure that Esther James was not on board.

Soon both buses were gone.

Esther James had to be in the building! For some reason, they could not enter the building. Frustrated, they began breaking windows yet they couldn't crawl through. Another agent attempted to use his car and smash through the church doors but, again, to no avail. For some reason they could not enter.

At the Whitehouse, Fred Joiner received word that the FBI had located Esther James and were on the verge of apprehending her. Fred wanted more information before going to McChellan. He knew what was at stake and what would happen to him if he disappointed the President again. Fred called the FBI and spoke directly with the head field agent on scene as to what their concerns were. Fred then hurried into the oval office to inform the President.

"Sir we found her! But . . ."

Looking up at Fred with disgust in his eyes, "But what?"

Fred stood back to regain his composure, "Sir, she is hold up in an old Pentecostal church in South Town. However, there is one problem."

To Fred's relief, McChellan simply rested back into his easy chair and calmly replied "Alright Fred, how can I help."

"Sir, for some reason the FBI cannot enter the building. They removed the doors and they still could not walk through the entrance!"

McChellan went from calm to having a violent tantrum in a matter of seconds. "It's him!" he roared, "He's helping them!"

"Who sir?"

"Why Fred, our true adversary! Fred, we will need the help from D.C. metro on this one, I'm sure they will be more effective."

McChellan knew many of D.C.'s finest were not yet infected and innocence could enter the building without resistance. Perhaps now he will finally have her, the one he knew held the power in her hands to destroy him.

Fred hurried from the room as fast as he could. McChellan had become a loose wire waiting to ignite and burn everything and everyone in his path, and he didn't want it to be him. Within minutes sirens came roaring down the street. Two black and whites drove into the parking area and stopped next to the black sedans parked in front. Fran Staples watched from a window inside waiting for her next move. She knew her instructions and she was ready.

Four metro police officers walked to the building, and they began talking to Pastor Hayes. Pastor Hayes calmly invited only two of the four officers into the building. They entered the building without resistance, increasing the anger of the FBI agents.

The press core began to arrive. Using their cell phones, they began reporting to their respective stations. The terrorists had been cornered by the FBI and would soon be in custody. It was curious that the FBI was standing by while the local police walked freely into the building.

All eyes were on that front door. Thirty minutes had passed. Finally, the two officers emerged from the front door escorting a young woman and an average size man in handcuffs. Both were dressed in long grey sweatshirts with their hoods tied tightly around their faces to hide their identities. Slowly, they walked toward the rear of the police car. The FBI agents tried to intercede by forming a ring of men around the black and white. Two of the agents approached the commanding officer and argued, that jurisdiction belonged to the federal government. They were there to take custody of the prisoners no matter how it needed to be done! The tone in their voices seemed almost threatening. However, the commanding police officer stood his ground. Insisting that any further discussion should be held out of the media's eye, Really meaning, "*do you know who's watching right now?*" All the arguing in the world between the two sides wasn't going anywhere, but it did force the attention of the agents off the others and onto him, taking their eyes off the other police officers, who was quietly putting the prisoners into the back seat of the squad car. Tired of the arguing, and seeing that the others was secured, the commanding police officer turned his back on the two agents and bulled his way to the drivers seat of his squad car and left.

The FBI agents were not happy. They knew the President needed her put some place far away from him, where no one could reach her. That certain precinct was only two blocks from the Whitehouse and that was way too close. The FBI agents climbed into their cars and followed the black and white units down the street. This was the closest they had ever gotten to apprehending Esther, and there she was, just within their grasp. They needed to get their hands on her and now.

Pastor Hayes walked somberly back into his office, then placed a call to Pastor Adams on his cell phone.

"They're on their way!"

"All is ready on this side Hayes, now it's up to God!"

Pastor Hayes, being the man of God that he was, began thinking about scripture immediately. God's word always gave him comfort and strength when he was stressed. He really wanted all he could get. "We really need to place all our trust in him now. I have an idea, Adam's, please, open your bible with me to the book of proverbs chapter 13, and let's read together verse 5, *"Every word of God is pure! He is a shield unto them that put their trust in him.* I don't know about anyone else Adams, but I believe that would be a great idea right about now!"

CHAPTER 26

Racing down 13th street the police cars soared with their sirens blaring. The black sedans were right behind them almost bumper to bumper forcing other cars off the road.

The FBI wanted Esther James and they were willing to do whatever it took to get her away from the local police.

The officer driving the transport car glanced to his left and noticed that one of the federal cars had sped past them. It was racing down a side street in an effort to get in front.

The officer driving stepped on the accelerator and sped up, determined not to be cut off further down the road. Now there were six cars racing at high speed toward the downtown area.

Suddenly, one of the two Federal cars that were behind them, moved up next to the driver's side of the squad car. It was followed by a second car that pulled up quickly and began pushing the squad car from behind, not allowing it to slow down.

Just up ahead the young officer noticed two large school buses parked directly in their path. The two federal cars were not going to allow him to move or slow down. Knowing that if they hit the bus at the speed they were going, not only would they be killed, but the people on the bus would be killed as well.

The officer needed to do something fast. Without concern for their own safety, the officer decided to turn directly into the front of the black sedan, slamming into the car's right quarter panel. The driver hit it over and over until a small opening appeared allowing him to speed up just enough to get around the school bus just slightly scraping the side of the bus with the right side mirror ripping it off the car.

Suddenly, the officer's partner shouted a warning as a large black object came from the left, hurling at high speed. The black sedan collided directly into the left side of the police car causing it to flip onto the vehicles side. The police car proceeded to slide another sixty feet scraping the concrete and creating massive sparks that flew into the air from underneath the body of the car.

Finally the car came to a stop. The four remaining Federal cars screeched to a stop and rushed back to the scene.

When they arrived, fifty or more young people surrounded the turned over police car all wearing grey sweatshirts. Each person had their hoods up and tied. All could have easily fit Esther's description.

The FBI agents frustrated by all the interference, rushed into the crowd pulling down hoods and brutally shoving people to the concrete until they reached the squad car. They stood baffled and very angry. The police officers were there, but their suspect was nowhere to be seen. Only a pair of opened handcuffs remained and hung from a metal bar that crossed the back seat but, no Esther James.

Fran walked away stiffly from the scene. Loosening her sweatshirt as she walked to the nearest bus stop. "*Wow, I did it*, she thought, *thank God I'm still alive*. Fran began to pray, perhaps, for the first time honestly, and with a humble heart. Thanking God for their lives, the mission, and for her friend Clarence Banks, after all, she got poor Clarence into this mess to begin with. Never had she placed her life in danger before, especially for a cause. This was well worth it.

The FBI continued running up and down the street stopping everyone who wore a hooded sweatshirt but there were so many.

The officers struggled to get out of the police car and stood to their feet. They were a little stunned but, O.K for the most part. Noticing that the agents were preoccupied with all the youth on the street, they turned nonchalantly from the crowd and began walking toward the nearest exit which, happily, was a nearby alley. Both the officers were concerned about the whereabouts of the two they had in the back seat. Clarence was a little frightened before all this began but, one could only guess how he was at this moment. The two knew they had to find him. Turning the corner, they entered into the ally, and walked slowly, hoping to get some hint of where Clarence was hiding.

Appearing from a dark area behind a row of cars, the outlined figure of a man emerged and cautiously walked toward the two police officers. "I don't understand how anyone could be so lucky? They never recognized you!" Clarence expressed joyfully. As the three embraced, the moment had to be short lived. There was just enough time for a short prayer to thank God for getting them through the crash alive.

"Here is where I leave you, said the commanding officer. It's up to you two now. I need to get back and have answers for all this! Best of luck."

Clarence Banks and Esther took their opportunity and left the area fast. Their walk became a run and soon the sound of sirens and yelling was behind them.

"We made it! Clarence, we made it! Stop for a moment and catch your breath"

"Esther, I never expected to get hit like that. I thought we were going to die!"

"Remember Clarence who is watching over us! We have got to finish this! So many are counting on us."

Gaining his confidence back, he checked his wristwatch, "Esther we only have thirty minutes to get this done. If we're going to do this, we had better hurry." They both turned and began walking the longest two blocks of their lives.

Up in his office, McChellan paced back and forth across the oval office. He wanted Esther James locked up or dead. She was just out of his reach and it was driving him to the point of insanity.

"Fred, get in here now!"

Fred left his desk and hurried into McChellan's office, "Yes sir!"

"I want increased reinforcements around this building! and do it fast!"

Fred froze for a moment "Do you mean the White-house?"

"You heard me! Get people here now! Use the military if you have to"

Fred returned to his desk out of breath from all the chasing he had been doing for McChellan. *More security? Why would he need so much more security? Especially for one little girl,* he thought. *"Why is he so afraid of her?*

Esther and Clarence knew their one advantage was the darkness. The streetlight above the alley was burnt out giving them a small amount of protection but was it enough?

Reaching the end of the alley, Clarence noticed that the stonewall in front of the school building stood out just long enough for them to hide behind.

"Esther, we need to see how many people they have guarding the place." The two crept along the side of the building until they reached the corner. Poking his head around the corner, he waited until the man standing guard at the front gate lit up his cigarette. Then the two, both on hands and knees, crawled behind that old stonewall. Both of them sat nervously anticipating what came next! Somehow they needed to cross the street and enter the building. Time was running out.

"We have fifteen minutes Esther, any ideas?"

"Clarence, I am dressed as a cop, and there is always the chance they still haven't been informed yet of who we are!" Clarence decided on one more look, rolling onto his stomach he looked around the edge of the wall. He noticed eight more men filling in at each door and all were carrying automatic weapons. Now came more trouble. Another military vehicle arrived dropping off twelve more personnel to surround the mass of people worshipping on the eastern side of the building.

"Nuts!" was all Clarence could say. "Still want to do this?" Esther grabbed him by the shirtsleeve and began pulling him toward the street, "Come on, what's a little jail time! Remember who is really in charge of this thing."

"I can't see down the alley" whispered Clarence, "but I'll bet they have people down there as well." Suddenly, Esther noticed a small light no larger then the tip of a pencil eraser moving back and forth behind some bushes on the opposite side of the building, "Clarence maybe that's our way in."

Agreeing on their next step, they retreated and moved back behind the old school building. After regrouping they began walking normally toward the street. "Esther, remember you're just a cop."

They walked out in plain view and began walking side-by-side making their way down the street until they reached the sidewalk.

Two of the FBI agents immediately left their posts and hurried straight toward them but, they remained calm and just waved. The two men noticed the police uniform and stopped, acknowledged them, then returned to their posts.

Now they were on the opposite side of the street and what's more, they knew that word hadn't spread yet that Esther was disguised as a cop!

Now beaming with confidence, the two began a long walk past the front of the building. Reaching the end of the street they felt as if they passed the first test.

"I don't believe it!" She whispered, "Ready for round two he asked with a smile. "All right, but we still need to get into that building."

"Did you still see that light?"

"No, but I do see a way we can reach that area!"

The two began climbing the fence and walked cautiously through the grounds until they reached the tall stonewall that separated the living quarters and Lincoln Hall. Esther climbed to the top of the wall and took a moment to look for security. Once again she noticed the small light shining. This time it was coming from a dark crevice along side of the building. Helping Clarence up to the top of the wall the two jumped down and hurried to the side of the building. They began walking cautiously to where Esther saw the light.

Suddenly a hand reached out and grabbed Esther from behind. Then, a second hand came round and covered her mouth to prevent her from screaming. Clarence turned to help but stopped short when he saw the two embracing.

"Please, Clarence," the stranger whispered, "I'm here to help. Look, there's not much time he looked at her, then at Esther, realizing that Esther must know her from somewhere.

"Hello, Clarence, my name is Jill Rafferity. Pastor Adams asked if I could be of some assistance, so I'm here to help!"

The darkness of the corner hid them well from the streetlights, making it easier to talk. Now remember what I'm about to tell you. It's what you will need to know to complete this mission. Without it, you will fail. Do you understand?"

"There are two officers standing guard around McChellan's office where he and Holland are waiting out the election. You will need to be able to exchange a certain code in order to be able to relieve those guards. I believe that this code will work." With that she slipped a small peace of paper into Esther's hand. "My source is good."

"Do you mean, it may not work?" asked Clarence.

"We have to do this Clarence. What choice do we have?"

Jill opened the side door to the tunnel then looked back at them. "Quick, change into these security uniforms. They're Whitehouse issued. Remember the code! Know it well, and say it with confidence. They will pick up on it if you show any hesitation. There's not much time, get moving!"

Clarence and Esther each took a deep breath and entered the tunnel. It was dark and the hallway was filled with old water logged boxes, stuff that had been stored there for years.

The two walked slowly down the hall climbing over the boxes, trying to be as quiet as possible, which was difficult with the sound of broken glass under their feet. A light was shinning from behind an old door that was hidden by a wall of desks.

Clarence quietly pushed aside the desks, giving them access to the doorway and proceeded into the building. Thank God no one was in sight! So he whispered back into the door way and summoned Esther.

The two walked toward the eastern part of the Whitehouse. So far no one was in sight. Maybe, just maybe, this might be easier then they thought! Then came the loud voice they dreaded to hear come from behind them.

"Halt! Identify yourselves!" The shout was loud and with authority.

Strong apprehension gripped them both, but they remained confident. "We are here to replace you!" replied Esther.

The guard looked behind the old door, which was still slightly opened.

"Why didn't you use the front entrance?" He replied sounding somewhat annoyed!

Calmly, Esther explained that they were trying to get past all the irritating people that were blocking the area. They found it easier to avoid the whole mess by simply coming in through the old entrance!

"This is our first time here. We didn't know that this entrance wasn't being used anymore."

She sounded convincing but he still had doubts. He escorted them to the front security desk.

Esther saw the office they wanted on the right side of the main hallway. Two large men stood guard on each side of the door.

When the three reached the front desk, Esther grew alarmed at what she saw. There were three other guards sitting at the desk, all of whom turned and looked directly at them.

Clarence began to panic. Esther gently placed her hand upon his back for assurance and then proceeded to the desk. The men looked menacing. For some reason none of them held any expression on their faces and that really creeped Esther out. "Here!" she said in a demanding tone. "The code!"

For Esther and Clarence this was the moment of truth.

Esther rattled off a series of numbers, then stood back to see if Jill had been right. "Alright, I guess if you have the code." replied the guard sounding almost disappointed. This man still didn't trust them.

Esther and Clarence walked over to the guards at the door and again she had to repeat the code. The two men stepped down and walked away from the door leaving Esther and Clarence just feet off their objective.

Esther and Clarence stepped up on the platform and turned facing the other guards trying to look menacing.

Esther watched as the two guards began walking toward the exit doors keeping one eye on them and one eye on the clock. She only had one minute left.

The phone began to ring. Esther watched the remaining guards at the desk as if impending doom was about to strike. It was no longer apprehension. Now it was down right fear and it began to take over. Something wasn't right. *Why were they looking at us like that?*

"It's them!" One of them shouted. The guard slammed down the phone and yelled, "Come on let's get them." The guards jumped from their seats and hurried toward Esther and Clarence.

Esther quickly stepped in front of the door and placed her hand on the coded key lock placed just above the doorknob. Esther's hands were visibly shaking as she made two feeble attempts to gain entry. On her third try, she heard the click she needed to hear and a small amount of relief entered her body, giving her the strength to continue. Esther placed her hands on the doorknobs and began to turn them, but they would not turn. To her dismay, the door would not open. The door had a second lock.

Clarence knew what he had to do no matter the consequences. With all his strength he ran toward the oncoming men and leapt into them, blocking them with his body.

"Hurry, Esther!" He screamed as the men viciously began to man handle him.

Just beyond the door McChellan sat at his desk clenching his fists. His eyes were black and cold. His facial expression was red hot with anger. He knew something was happening outside his door, but he felt powerless to stop it. For some reason his mind was being blocked. Holland looked out the window with great concern. Was what he was feeling coming from that large group of young people or from outside in the hall? All he knew just then was that it tore from within, more powerful than ever before. It had become more than he could bear.

Then a loud pounding came from outside the door. All at once their eyes were opened to what was happening. Holland couldn't stand the torment any longer. He knew who was coming and there was no stopping him. Holland reached up and grabbed his ears in an attempt to block the words that continued to penetrate his very being. Holland just gasped in surrender and dropped to his knees.

Starting out as in a low moan, McChellan began to move and twist in his chair, clenching his fists swinging them over and over wildly in all directions.

Then in a last attempt of expressing his tormented rage McChellan gave out a final scream.

"She's going to do it! Blast! He's going to win again!"

Just then the door to his office crashed open. Clarence, along with two of the Whitehouse security staff, came tumbling through the door onto the floor. McChellan stood to his feet as Esther James hurried through right behind them, and gently placed God's word down on his desk right before his eyes, with one second to go!

McChellan now weak and limp, struggled in his attempt to reach Esther, but the words she was speaking pierced his heart like a two edged sword. Wearily, McChellan fell to the floor. On the other side of the desk Esther stood with her hands raised high, reciting scripture and praising God like never before. Esther's body actually began to illuminate the room.

Marcus was in torment. He began slamming his fists against the window glass that had been such a useful tool for the past four years, but now shattered from the fierce force behind his blows. Clarence embraced Holland with a strong bear hug so no further harm could be afflicted to his body and held him tight.

Then, just as fast as the demon entered into these men, it left. Clarence watched in awe as McChellan crawled his way back to Marcus Holland to help him with the cuts on his hands. The guards got up off the floor as if they had no idea as to what had just taken place. Taking his trembling bleeding hands away from his face, Marcus Holland looked up to behold the woman he loved, with a glow upon her face that only God could have provided.

Seeing the Bible on the desk the two men's eyes were opened to the sin they were in. They fell to their faces and began to worship God, and repent.

Esther and Clarence walked calmly through the french doors out onto the balcony. As soon as Pastor Hayes saw them he knew the victory had been won. He and the other three Pastors rushed from the crowd, past the outside security and joined the two upstairs.

Shelly and Tom saw the event and with camera in hand followed close behind. As Shelly and Tom approached the room, Shelly began to quiver and tremble. Entering the room both stood in awe witnessing a warm, soft glow that engulfed the room. Peace like they never felt before covered them. Tom just about dropped his camera in disbelief. The Pastors were praying fervently over the former President and Vice President. Esther was standing with her arms raised and singing as if in a foreign language. Tom couldn't understand a word of it. Then of all things unheard of, Tom watched as his reporter and friend, fell to her knees and began sobbing as well. Tom felt out of place and decided to go out on the balcony. On the way out there came a sound never heard since the days of Azusa Street, and it was happening outside. Tom walked slowly as if his legs wouldn't move. For some reason, he really didn't want to leave the room. It was so peaceful in there. The joy he was feeling, he wanted to keep.

Reaching the railing, Tom looked out over the eastern side of the Whitehouse grounds. Two thousand people were on their knees, worshiping God. Hundreds more just stood and sobbed speaking out in languages undiscernable as the Holy Ghost fell upon them all. Tom raised the camera to catch the action. Never had he ever felt anything like it before. Tom filmed what he could for the nightly news and then returned to the room only to witness yet another miracle. Esther James and Marcus Holland were embracing and acknowledging their love for each other. Tom knew something great happened that day, he saw a miracle.

CHAPTER 27

Within months after God's great victory, the nation as a whole began flourishing again. For the moment, the creature's influence wasn't guiding the land.

There were two new people sitting in the Whitehouse taking control almost immediately. President Morrison, on his very first day in office ordered investigations into all the people involved in the great conspiracy.

Shelly Cleveland and her cameraman Tom Jacobs, had become famous within the media circuits. Not only did they have the exclusive story about Esther James, they were also on hand for the arrest of Jack Mason as he was escorted in handcuffs from Aztec Motors. Later, Shelly interviewed Frank B. Ashford while in prison awaiting his trial. Nasaki Yuhma was replaced as CEO of the Asian Motor Group at the strong urging of President Morrison and sent back to the Chinese.

Inside the Senate, Vice President Peeling took charge of the investigation of all the congressmen and senators that had a role in the now unsuccessful take over of our government. The most popular were Senator Ben Cross and Senator Agnes Whiting who protested for hours while being questioned. Their attorney's proclaimed their innocence by reason of insanity. It seemed funny to the media that they both claimed to have had no memory of what they were doing the past four years.

It was a time of peace and tranquility in the country. Companies began to flourish, as did employment. Factories increased production, sparking off, massive hiring throughout the land.

Morrison ordered that the accounts from within Ashford Investments be opened, forcing the firm to return as much money as possible to the retirement accounts that had money stolen while under the McChellan administration. The smaller investment firms followed and, soon after, Wall Street was back on track. Food prices began to lower, property taxes lowered as did interest rates on loans making it easier for people to afford homes. Companies no longer were hit with unreasonable tax rates helping them prosper here and not over seas.

The people found a new hope for their future. The church's plan of rescue was now in action. Homeless shelters and food pantries sprang up throughout all of the D.C. area helping the people that still needed a safe place to sleep, or until a new job came their way. The youth that had come on the scene just before Election Day were again in action, but in a different way. These young people created educational classes to teach the homeless to find confidence and build self-esteem, everything they needed, before going into a job interview. They held evening services anywhere they could find an empty place to gather. Christ's Sword church was always one of those places.

One evening, Pastor Hayes received a visit from Shelly Cleveland and Tom Jacobs. Tom still had many questions that something deep inside of him needed to know.

"You see Tom, four years ago, it was Esther who was the first to see the creature for what it was and in whom it was living. She was chosen by God to be the deliverer of His word. God knew Esther's heart, and the love she carried for Marcus. That love made her ideal for His use. God's word had to be held in her hand and delivered by her, at a certain time. The evil one arrived at a time of government transition, or if you wish, at election time. Unlike God, satan is not omnipresent. He actually has to show up himself to make his plans effective. God chose that specific time to fulfill his plan. Did you notice, Tom, that I said *His* time? It's never ours! It wasn't until after lengthy intercessory prayer, God revealed to me a plan and it had to be followed exactly.

By the look on your face Tom, you really don't buy that explanation."

"I know what I saw and what I felt. What was that glow I saw and that feeling? I never felt anything like it!"

Shelly smiled brightly and replied, "It was God! Tom, I know it was God! The Holy Spirit filled the room but Pastor, does God always appear that way?"

"Not always so majestically Shelly, but you always know He's there. Remember, He promised to never leave or forsake you so you know he is always there. Remember too, that we had been praying non-stop for four years, the prayer power outside the Whitehouse was pretty strong. I feel blessed He chose to visit us the way he did. Not everyone has a chance to experience Him the way you did. God has always loved you, but now, you know Gods grace and the love He has for you.

"I loved what I felt Pastor, how can I feel that way again?" replied Tom. Pastor Hayes took Tom by the arm and they excused themselves from the room.

"Son, let's you and I have a little talk."

Shelly remained behind and began to pray. Slowly she lifted her arms high toward heaven; then she quietly whispered, "To God be the glory."

FINAL THOUGHT

In Ephesians 6:12 Paul said, "For we wrestle not against flesh and blood, but against principalities, against powers, against the rulers of darkness of this world, against spiritual wickedness in high places."

Every day, all around us, we see the atrocities people do to themselves and to others. The daily newspaper is consistently reporting incidents regarding young people, feeling the need to use a gun on another, because of bullying.

Greedy public officials, who, when entrusted with other peoples money, become tempted, and eventually get caught stealing.

Drug addicts, become panic stricken when they lose their employment, usually due to drugs. These same people then have to resort to stealing in order to satisfy their addiction.

Some people find themselves killing others for something as simple as a piece of clothing.

In this book, I tried to bring these dark spirits into view. McChellan and Holland sought power. The demon simply shaped their attitudes and created the monsters they eventually became. The only thing that saved them was the Word of God.

Think about the last time you lashed out in anger. Our flesh and the lusts of this world can cause great affliction in the family unit. Sometimes bouncing back from our mistakes requires a little more than just an apology. Try picking up your bible and reading it. God's word is powerful and will help you triumph over any obstacle that may be in front of you.

As America keeps moving away from God, one can plainly see how the devils minions are finding homes so easily. Remember who we are really fighting against when making choices. It's not always the person, but the things of darkness that reside within.

BIBLE REFERENCES

All verse references are from the King James Bible.

1. Romans 1:21-25, 28-29.
2. Psalms 91:11, Luke 4:10.
3. Mark 5: 2-9.
4. Psalms 7:9.
5. Colossians 1:9-10.
6. Matthew 25:35.
7. Acts 1:14.
8. Acts 2:38.
9. Acts 10.
10. Romans 8.
11. Acts 1:12-14.
12. Acts 2:1-4.
13. Ephesians 6:12.
14. Proverbs 13:5.

Your local UPCI can be found in the yellow pages or visit our website at www.upci. org.